The Tales of Barnacle Bill

SKELETON KREWE
(CHRONICLE II)

The Tales of Barnacle Bill

SKELETON KREWE (CHRONICLE II)

Barnacle Bill Bedlam

Doce Blant Publishing

www.DoceBlantPublishing.com

Published by

Doce Blant Publishing, Dana Point, CA 92629

www.doceblantpublishing.com

Cover Design: Fiona Jayde Media

Interior Images: T. Kirby, Barnacle Bill Trading Co.

ISBN: 978-0-9967622-2-9

Printed in the United States of America

Dedicated to Sharoda J. Snyder

Although I feel I spent a good bit of our time as a burden, it never meant I didn't love you. Truth be known, I loved you the most.

You entrusted me with the life of your only daughter. You saw the man in me that I wanted to be and for that I am forever grateful. I cannot fill the void of a life lost or a wound that will not heal.

Makes me wonder, will there ever be redemption for the bereaved, worthy enough to save faith, and strong enough to save a heart? Only God knows why. At fifty four I still sit and wonder.

So when your spirit starts to soar, I hope you think of me, smile, and know that your little girl is safe and happy in the hands of love – then, now, and forever more... just as I promised.

I will take heart in the gift of knowing that I was the last one to hold your hand.

This book is dedicated to your memory.

So long Memmy ... I'll see you on the horizon!

Love always, B

To Sharon
Fair Winds & Good
Fortune always

Acknowledgments

I acknowledge that I am NOT of sound mind …
nor have I ever been, I'll not lie to you!
My childish years live on to this day in so many ways.

Ask anyone I know, in spirit or in body.
They'll say the man is daft. A boat with no oar.
But I do have passion … for life and all it has to offer.

Mark Twain once said:
"Twenty years from now you will be more disappointed by the things that you did not do than by the ones you did. So throw off the bow lines, sail away from the safe harbor, catch the trade winds in your sails, explore, dream and discover."

Here's to your Dreams!

contents

Prologue

A Second in Time

DREADFUL IS THE BOND ONE CARRIES laced in regret. Gemstones - pivotal moments in one's life, be it for love or money. A meager glance, an instant that with a spoken word would've changed the course of destiny...your direction, maybe even the direction of all mankind.

Monumental moments that were passed upon due to weakness or indecision, a second in time that will never come again.

Some wear old memories like war wounds. Others, in solemn times, will immerse themselves in sorrow and retrospect of a life that could have been.

A sad song, with so many people, so many lives that live for the past. For them it's hard to see what awaits just beyond the horizon. Or, as dear old Grandpa used to say, "Ya can't see the rainbow for the rain!"

Chapter 1

Old Habits Die Hard

FORTUNATELY FOR ME THAT WAS NEVER A worry.

Regret is a foolish emotion that I refuse to serve. Regret implies decision, the choice, while standing at the crossroads of life. And if the tea may be told, my decisive nature has relied solely on one thing… reckless abandon.

No fault of mine of course.

So, as I sit atop this rickety ol' sea post fence at the crossroads of *my* life, I am once again faced with "the choice." Once more I bear the resemblance of the boy in the looking glass. A few years older but none the wiser, I assure you.

On one side of the fence, the warm crystal blue waters of Mother Ocean are glistening in the sun. The other side hosts the cobblestone streets of a life I once knew. I feel a tear run down my face but I keep my smile, waiting for the winds of change to blow me off of this fence in one direction or another… so full of life I was.

From here I can see the people on 18th Street—a

picturesque world as they move along in their separate lives. As for me, time stands still. My reckless spirit is like a Lazy Susan, here they come… here come those feelings again! Could these feral reflections be something effortless as an itch in need of a scratch? Or is it another pathway on my road to oblivion? Either way I'm called to laugh at the absurd notions of an unbalanced mind. One thing's for sure… I gotta keep myself away from me!

Suddenly the serene sound of the white cap waves is overshadowed by a single voice riding on the wind. "You there, Boy! Might I trouble you for some assistance?" It echoes across the sand. With a modest nod and very few manners left in these bones, I climb from the fence to the aid of a stranger.

Cloaked in obscurity, this elderly woman steps from the shadows like a ghost into a fog, unnoticed and unaware… at first. Her wretched and destitute appearance has the locals up in arms in short time. The ignorance of the townspeople comes to life as they amuse themselves to the stranger with disregard. My faith in mankind once again takes a blow.

Now, I have the blood of a pirate and at times, a mouth the size of a crocodile.

I was blazin' to shout out in a rage, "We're All children of God and her blood is just as red as yours Sir!" But to avoid confrontation I kept my big mouth shut and we moved along our merry way. Ignorance as such is an abomination of man, I have no stomach for it. If I had a vessel and a bay of cannons, this village would be in my crosshairs by now! It becomes more and more apparent that I got off on the wrong side of the fence.

The stranger was burdened with one too many bags to carry by herself, and did so with a sympathetic limp. She said she wasn't going far. I picked up as many bags as I could possibly carry and we began to push on. I noticed in walking that she favored her right hip and could only move so fast due to the pain – a victim of age.

She was outfitted in a rather large brown cloak with an oversized hood that shielded her face from the sun and from the public eye. I guess I can see why some would be under suspicion when crossing her path. Even I have yet to see her likeness. It looked like something akin to a monk's or priest's robes, the garb of a man of God. I found it peculiar, being (the fact) that it's a warm summer's day. I even asked her why at this time of season "would you make that the garment of choice?" I could hear her snicker then she simply said, "at the time it was all I could afford."

We moved along 18th Street at a snail's pace and to be honest, the bags weren't getting any lighter! But I kept my composure and continued on because it was I that had offered to help, and I'm a man of my word.

She was quite the conversationalist. Indeed, she had the gift of gab. Frankly I don't think many people in her past have given her the time or the stage to share her musings and she was all bottled up. Sad really.

It wasn't long into our walk before I found

myself growing more enthralled by her stories—so true to life. She reminisced of her existence by the sea and her son, the one source of all of her pride. She boasted that he was an admiral in the fleet of the Queen's Navy and how he would shower her with gifts from different ports of call—trinkets and treasures that he had acquired on his travels.

So what was it that brought our walk of words to a standstill? She then confessed of the manner in which he died. She raved of an infamous battle he had led and a dramatic firefight with bloodthirsty pirates. She described the scene in great detail as if she were there. Her words were so vivid in color that I felt I could reach out and touch them.

Then with a timely pause she spoke. "Their ship... it was swallowed by the sea and with it, it's captain." She still remembered the hour, the moment, and the letter left for her by a faceless courier. The letter of regret from the Queen's hand to hers. Telling her that her son would not be coming home. 'A life lost in honor and good service'. It said nothing more.

Every day, when the tide is high, she makes her way alone down this desolate street to this very harbor. She takes her place on this bench and feeds the seagulls, never taking her eyes off the horizon. She sits patiently watching. With every new day there's hope. Hope that one day she will see his sails. She sits and prays for his return but it never comes. She carries the letter with her to this day in remembrance of her good son. I never uttered a word. I could only feel her pain.

The sun had reached it's peak as we stopped for a breath and a glance. I must admit I love those crystal clear days when you can look to the skies and see the sun and moon looking down. Aside from it's natural beauty, it makes for calm waters and a smooth sail.

So captivated by her voice I was that I never took notice—we had arrived at our destination. The reason I knew was because I could feel the hairs on my arms begin to stand up. My good deed was met, yet I was still caked in sweat—feeling like I was covered in a blanket of apprehension as I found my feet at the end of 18th Street, where it meets Alligator Alley.

In a sudden daze, I heard voices of old souls, whispers in the wind... calling to me. Strange. Slowly I turned, step by step, inch by inch, as it were. And there it was... I couldn't believe it!

The old woman must have thought I was daft as I stood there frozen to the bone with eyes like turtle eggs and a mouth full of flies. She was just how I remembered her, it was a place that I knew well. It was Sadie's place. I was back at the Ol' Mill Tavern.

Stricken in my moment of confusion and awe, I begin to stutter and mumble under my breath the only words that I could muster, "The blood of a pirate runs deep here," I said, my words slurring as I spoke.

It was then and there when the old woman decided to remove the shroud that covered her face and head, exposing herself to the world… and to me. Why, this woman wasn't scary, she wasn't disfigured or grimacing in any way! She looked like what I assume that my grandmother would have looked like, had I ever met her. She looked me in the eye and displayed a subtle smile that revealed her kindness and good nature.

"Old habits die hard."

Immediately I started in with a usual barrage of questions, as I always do whenever I'm nervous, uncomfortable, or in a tight spot!

"How do you know this place, why are we here?" I said, suffering in my state of anxiety.

She told me that she had come to help a friend who was down on her luck. Said she was renting a flop on the second floor and would be staying until she was back on her feet and that the moderate supplies that we carried were for her. I silenced myself in worry and wondered about an old friend, trying my best not to let the stranger know that I too shared the blood of a Pirate.

She asked if I would "be a dear and grab the remaining things" and follow her inside. I paused reluctantly while trying to build up some courage. I knew that once I passed through those doors I would be off and beyond, doing something foolish and unheard of like... chasing a dream—never knowing when or even *if* I would return!

I blamed it on my thick skull and childlike stupidity as I took a deep breath and sighed then grabbed the remaining bags and proceeded to follow her in. The moment I set foot inside, I could hear the planks in the old wood floor beneath me creak with memories. Nothing had changed... no barstool moved, no glass overturned. It was how it stayed in my memory and if memory serves, my last visit here was a prosperous one! I had a hot plate of steak and potato lined with gold as I sat at the favorite barstool of an infamous pirate!

Yes, it's the one in front of the mirror by the kitchen door. I begin to point, "it's that one right th..." And before I could get the word *there* out of my mouth something caught my eye that sent me into a tailspin! I saw it and begin to pant.

Sitting on the bar in front of that very same barstool that I spoke of was a hot plate covered with a stainless steel top, just like the one that was locked in my mind forever. Was it true? Could it be real? Could this be happening to me all over again? I had that strange feeling that I was once again... lost in time!

Chapter 2

Spearhead

WITHOUT SO MUCH AS A SAD ATTEMPT TO finish my sentence, I started to slither my way towards the bar like a low-bellied snake with its mouth foaming. There wasn't a soul in the place, so none the wiser, eh? I had to see what lie beneath that stainless steel top. It was the pirate in me!

Just then a voice bellowed from the kitchen, "Georgia My Dear, where have the winds been keepin' ya? Your meal's gettin' cold!"

From beyond the door burst Sadie in all her glory. Sadie, or what was left of her. It seems she had been the victim of an accident. Her left cheek was swollen and bruised, her eye was black. She had her left arm in a sling, as it was broken.

I felt a tear comin' as I remembered her as an old friend—one of the strongest ladies I had the pleasure of knowing. Her wardrobe was as stylish and fashionable as her wit. But the Sadie I saw before me looked tattered and torn. The fiery gleam in her eye it seemed had burned out. She didn't see me at first and merely walked through the kitchen door past the bar. That's when I caught her eye. Her warm smile shielded her pain but couldn't hide the tears that followed when she first saw my face. With arms wide open I was welcomed back into her life.

Much to my surprise it *was* just a hot meal that Sadie had prepared for a friend in waiting. What a pity. Not a doubloon in sight.

Her name was Millicent Batiste LeVeau but she went by "Georgia." She told me it had been the pet name her late husband had used to "swear by" during their romance… quite funny. Through light conversation, I'd come to find that Georgia and Sadie both served together as missionaries some twenty years ago on the Island of Anguilla, four miles south of Saint Maarten in the Caribbean.

For reasons of her own choosing, Sadie did not offer to share with me the nature of her injuries. My answers came a short while later when I overheard the murmurs from the kitchen. From my knowledge, it was apparent that throughout the years, many a pirate's cache had been cut in that kitchen. I kept my ear bent eagerly for pieces of the puzzle… something I could use.

Sadie's unpleasant wounding was by the compliments of The Company, as it were. The Company was a "call name" for a squadron of mercenaries enlisted by the Queen, under the direction of Lord Alexander Willard. From what I gathered, Lord Willard was a sniveling wretch, underhanded and twice as devious. He became aware that Sadie had knowledge of a certain voyage undertaking and sent a ring down to convince her to tell all.

The next few minutes they shared in jeers and jabs at Lord Willard, then things got interesting. They spoke of a gathering of men, a voyage of unearthly proportion and the crazed Captain who dared guide this expedition. For some men I fear the world is not enough, they push the boundaries of their own humanity in search of that new realm. All is done in the name of conquest—weaving and winding their vessels beyond the horizon without the slightest notion of what they might find.

The grave details of this passage were not disclosed and I couldn't possibly press my ear against the door any harder without falling through. It looked as if I would be forced to dig a little deeper.

I begin the adventure with my usual turning of the stones. I made my way down to the pier looking for clues with an eye keen for the obvious: tall ships loading a lot of cargo as if for a steady departure and the like, but I found nothing, only shrimp boats cleaning their catch. After an hour or more of dead ends, I began to feel like a lost dog chasing his tail. I needed to cool off.

The sun became relentless, beating down on me. I had nothing to drink so I decided to take a respite on the edge of that dock and put my red blistered feet in the cool blue sea.

I flopped my bum down on the dock next to a lone fisherman talking to himself and whistling away. I swear, the moment I dunked my feet into the crystal blue waters I could hear them sizzle and hiss… yes, they were that hot!

Like the tide at my feet, it wasn't long before the conversation with himself started to float my way.

"The name's Ben Langley but everyone calls me Bilgewater or Bilgewater Ben," he told me proudly with a smile. "I'll be catching fireflies before fish this day," he said and the sarcasm in his voice was thick as molasses.

"No favorable bites, eh?" I inquired.

"Oh they're biting. They're eating like kings! They've stolen every shrimp from my line but I guess it is what I deserve because I stole them from the shrimper's down the way," he replied.

We talked of fishing and warm weather and the lovely array of ladies that passed us up and down the boardwalk. As I recall, I never introduced myself as I let the chat ramble on, so enthralled in his chatter, I was.

Finally he said, "So how will you be spending your day young sir?"

"Chasing my tail it seems," I said, laughing. My patience and subtle nature had worn thin so I started to pull threads. "I hear rumor of a ship taking on sailors for a voyage."

I took a few morsels of the talk between Sadie and Georgia and added my dramatic flair of experience and bull crap to convince him I knew what I spoke of, though in truth, I did not. Still, I must have touched a nerve in old Bilgewater because his cheerful smile disappeared from his face.

"The Voyage of Carbonados," he said with a ghostly look in his eye. "Foolish boy! You have so much life ahead of you. Walk away!" His eyes looked right through me as he attempted to cut me with his words. A man in motion, I grabbed my boots and did just that… walked away!

My ambition to make a quiet escape and not upset him was fouled, as I neared the end of the dock he beckoned me once more. "It's a Ransom you seek!" he cried out. I paused briefly for one last look back. "It's about an hour's walk south, you'll find her in Delves inlet," he said.

I continued on but the puzzled look on my face strengthened. His words haunted me: *It's a Ransom you seek!* Why did it trouble me? There was something stuck in my very soul, something familiar that I could not recall.

I was almost out of sight when old Bilgewater Ben shouted out his last, "And you'll steer clear of Morgan if you know what's good for you, boy," he laughed as he said it, shouting from across the bay. I must have only made it about ten more paces before the colors started to clear. Something from my past disturbed me.

"Ransom? Morgan?" Right then the tumblers inside my head fell into place. Could the Ransom in question be the ship, *A Pirate's Ransom?* A chill ran over me because my gut knew what would come next: its captain, one of the most fearsome rogues. His calling card was a polished brass hook in place of his left hand. I can still hear the chilling sounds of that hook as it scratched against the walls of my memory. I suspect it be the infamous Morgan the Hook. Suddenly my bright idea of adventure didn't seem so bright.

With the threat of the Hook looming near, my adventurous stride to Delves Inlet slowed to a Sunday's pace. *Take time, contemplate all decisions of what lie ahead,* I thought as the minutes passed. Just then, the ground beneath my feet turned to marsh as I drew nearer to the cove.

Shielded in seclusion, it was easy to understand why pillagers and pirates would make this their chosen place for a discreet dock. The trees and woodlands carried right up to the water's edge. With the *Ransom* still not in sight, my nervousness began to surface as I found myself being followed by snakes and the croaking chatter of alligators just behind my shoulder.

I fought my way through the thicket, moving upstream about a hundred yards. Traces of what appeared to be a crow's nest crested the treetops in the distance.

As I cut past the last bit of brush, the reason for that pit in my stomach came in to full view. Below sat the only ship of its kind—*A Pirate's Ransom,* burnt red in color with black and white striped sails. Quite garish for a pirate ship I must say, but Morgan the Hook's flamboyance was typically backed by a wall of cannon fire. This much I knew to be true… I'd seen it!

My knowledge comes from experience when speaking of the legend known as Morgan the Hook, it's both fierce and factual. His ruthless ways have put fear in the hearts of many a sailor… including me!

The perilous captain serves as monarch in a very elite group, a band of pirates that call themselves "The Brethren of Caroline." The core of their rebellion is comprised of three ships sailed by three Captains respectively. Alongside the Hook and his precious *Ransom,* you'll find it's sister ship *The Leucosia,* captained by an old friend, the villainous Robert "Bloody Bob" Carver.

And then there was one.

The Pirate King. The spearhead of this small army of rogues and rapscallions. A name I've become quite familiar with over the past. He saved my life once… twice actually! Although it's been several years, it seems like centuries ago. He's by far one of the most glorified pirates that I've come to know.

His name, Barnacle Bill Bedlam.

He captains a ship called *Calypso's Revenge,* a larger vessel in size and much more dominant than many I've seen. It is known as the mother ship of the BOC.

The Brethren of Caroline is just that… *brethren.* A large body of men *and* women fighting for their freedom and independence. Their name is notorious throughout the South. From the Caribbean waters to the Gulf of Mexico, their legend precedes them. But in this day and age, they fight for their lives as the Queen has tightened her stronghold on all that call themselves "pirate," and will stop at nothing to indemnify her reign.

My mind starts to wander. What was it that brought the Brethren's return to my little corner of the world and what be their intentions? Truth be known, they plan for sail as I watch them from the shoreline.

The water starts to rise as they begin to stow the massive ship. Nearly a dozen men in constant rotation from ship to shore, a bucket brigade of pirates. They brought boxes and barrels and burlap bags by the plenty, even livestock… and of course rum, least I forget!

The wheels in my head are spinning round and round. What mysteries lie on this cryptic Voyage of Carbonado? This I must know, I must find out!

Chapter 3

Into the Midnight Blue

WITHOUT THE SLIGHTEST INKLING OF where they'll venture, what they seek, or the dangers that wait for me, I am feeling overwhelmed. That reckless spirit has found me once more as I begin to ponder and conspire my way aboard. Remember, *thick skull and childlike stupidity.*

Oh, but there is one small hindrance to my master plan, a stumbling block if you will and that be Morgan the Hook! The wrath of Hook is boundless and bold. A chill falls over a room the moment he walks in. Familiar tales, familiar lies. A legacy of fear and retribution surrounds him—the man of many faces, perilous and shrewd.

Trying my best to remain privy, I work my way through the palms like a thief in the night, closer and closer to the ship with not a clue as to how I will infiltrate her. My plan to board and not get caught!

I waited in the wings for just the right wind to strike me. The clock in my head slowly turned, I could hear it ticking, ticking, driving me on. They say every road to glory begins with chance, a single roll of the dice.

The men scurried and scrambled like bees in a hive with much commotion and diligence. With astute timing I made my move, without warning, without fail. Weaving my way through the fray I struggled, tossing a sack of feed over my shoulder to appear part of the crew, then off I went.

Looking rather foolish, I found myself walking like a drunkard from the weight of the burlap sack bearing down on me. With every intent not to draw attention to myself I stumbled and wound down the long pier to where the *Ransom* lay waiting.

I was doing all I could do to keep up in line and prevent this heavy load from bringing me to my knees. "Whew, now I know why they call it a long pier," I joked to myself.

While crossing the gangplank to board I was overcome with a strange sense of irony. I felt like Jonah descending into the belly of the whale. With haste I tossed and shuffled about in transit, fighting my way to the ship's hold to store my carry. The business intensified as ship and krewe readied themselves to wander this world on the Voyage of Carbonados.

With an experienced history of playing the stowaway, I'll say that it is not recommended for the modest or sensible. Ill fate was certainly assured if found flirting on the wrong side of the Hook! I weaseled my way out of the order and out of sight as I began my feeble investigation of the ship, with the plan to avoid Morgan all in the same breath.

As dusk settled on this covert little inlet, my plan of attack was sure, albeit a loose one. Knowing, by the puzzled looks scattered about, it seemed I was not the only figure blind with knowledge of this mission. I decided I would wait 'til nightfall, time of retire, and gather at the gossip tables—every ship has one. It was located in the *"Focs,"* or forecastle of the ship (to you landlubbers). It is where the Krewe bunks. They drink, they sing, they share truths and lies amongst each other, reveling in their joys and woes. That would be the place where I would find my answers. So I kept to myself, waiting patiently for nightfall to arrive as we pointed the nose of this magnificent vessel into the heart of the midnight blue.

Prepping the ship was all but done yet we remained ghostly still. In lieu of wandering eyes from the nearby village, we waited for the black of night to silently slip away. One by one the men on deck dissipated, working their way down to the *focs* for a little social and drink. I waited 'til they got rather tipsy before I made my intrusion. Tight lips run loosely when the grog takes hold. But the clock was ticking. I must find my resolutions quickly or be trapped aboard with no turning back.

My heart beat heavy and my mind spun as the pressures of *the choice* consumed me. Yet I was still anonymous, just another face… I could still walk away.

The wait was over. I heard the dull roar of

their chants and hisses, the shanties, meaningless chatter, the clanking of tankards. A good time to slip in and so I did.

With a bit of luck I found my way in 'off-the-cuff', as it were. They paid me no mind at all. I took seat on a bag of feed near the center of the room and awaited the elders' confessions. The room was buzzing with strong drink and laughter. The cards were dealt, the pistols pulled as musicians played guitar in the corner, setting the mood for the evening. Then things began to unfold.

I noticed a small gathering two tables down from me, centered around a grey haired gent with blue eyes. A rather fancily dressed gent who went by the name of Turtle. The men kept to him, close as if they were following orders. He was a highwayman who sold tankards and flasks that he'd pull from his pockets, along with nicely carved pipes that he had whittled from bone.

His name was Brit Belvoir—familiar name to me. My father's sister carried the name Belvoir. As I understand it's religious and from the bible. It means "favored by God."

He was known as Turtle Brit by the krewe. They called him that because he used to fashion different things out of turtle shells for trade. He even wore a turtle skull on his hat. Items he carved cut a good cache but the thing he held highest in value for trade was information. He knew of the Voyage of Carbonados. Eyes of the curious scanned the room, never losing scope of the one called Turtle.

Although he's been known to cheat a man blind in a game of cards, Brit was a good spirit, of good heart so-to-speak, as he shared in the camaraderie. Rarely was he seen not wearing a smile. True to a pirate's soul, he lived for the day.

My suspicions rang true, the blue eyed gent held the key. But to this moment no words of fate were spoken. He held his tongue, giving an occasional nod to the door, apparently awaiting the arrival of certain ears. My nervous tic began to get the best of me.

Now we've all had our bouts with conscience – you know that little cretin that sits on your shoulder and breathes a smug *'I told you so'* whenever you slip from grace. I seldom wonder where those voices go when we do things for the good, prideful things, things of good merit. You'll not find them. No *'good job',* no pat on the back… not a whisper. Why that is? Perhaps it's not ours to know. It didn't matter because at this very moment my conscience was at its post, coming in loud and clear, warning me off the ship and the coming of fearful things.

I sat there silent and still as a bone grave, not moving forward, not turning back while the cretins of common sense drone on. If there's something to be found here, I must know what it is!

Suddenly the ever smiling Brit dropped his grin. He calmly put away his wares of trade and pulled out five small tin cups, one tucked inside the other. The mood of the room changed to black as he separated then set each tin cup atop the table position in front of a respective chair. The poor sods that had been sitting there quickly moved with nervous haste, freeing up seats the table. The man called Turtle then filled each cup from a flask he carried on his hip. The dull roar of the forecastle faded to murmur as I could hear bodies on the wooden gangplank coming this way. Too soon, the hour glass had all but emptied on the evenings shortcomings as the sounds of footsteps draw closer. I begin doing the bum bottom shuffle, inching my way back from where I sit, back into the shadows without notice, without a stir as two men filled the doorway.

With fearful eyes I could see them clearly—two strangers from a remembrance. These were two strangers that I knew oh so well. Although the *Ransom* remained anchored and still, my proverbial ship was all but sunk. It was a Pirate Lord, the Captain of the *Leucosia,* Bloody Bob Carver and his quartermaster, Hugh Jorgan.

These men know of me.

A bold captain it's true, noble and courageous but ornery as a snake. I'll just say our dealings in the past have been memorable ones, on the edge of lost control. I hold him in high regard, aside from the small insignificant fact that he loathes my smile and everything about me.

They share handshakes and cordials, squabble over long goodbye's, and then promptly take to their seats, awaiting the foretelling. Two seats remain empty.

Suddenly the distinct sound of a man's walk

commands the room. It echoes above me with depth from the old wooden planks. I hear the footsteps coming… coming for their place at the table.

I know that sound, I know that walk, I've heard it before, it lingers in my memory.

It was Morgan… and he's coming.

Morgan the Hook, the man I speak of in song and story. Captain of the *Pirates Ransom*—captain of the very ship that my narrow behind is falsely aboard. At best I'll be swinging from the mast come twilight.

Those minions of reason that chime in my ear begin to sound more reasonable as I start to rethink my possibilities with my eyes neatly focused on the door. I was shortly derailed in train of thought when I realized that I could no longer hear the footsteps, they fell silent. Yet no Hook. The doorway remained empty.

I heard the rudder creak, the ringing of chains drowns out—they're raising anchor. Time is a luxury I can ill afford!

Mix frivolous nature of adolescence with a bad sense of time and placement, and you'll find me, painting myself into a corner or a situation I can't control. In an instant my fears took a turn for worse.

Within a single breath the room faded to pitch black. Every flame, every candle, every match flickered once then went out in a puff of smoke as if on command, like some gust of wind that had passed through this closed-off room, taking every gleam of light with it. I felt nothing… no wind, no breeze. In fact, the air was so thick that it was hard to breathe.

The men fumbled for their matches, hoping the fire sticks would help them to see. Turtle Brit regained the light at the table with a novel device of his own creation. He called it his "Flintkicker" — a small handheld object that when squeezed in the palm of his hand, caused two flints to spark. The flash ignited a hemp-made wick that he had dipped in whale oil (there's quite a creative character behind this man). Only a handful got a chuckle over the Turtle's invention, most seemed reserved from the incident, a bit apprehensive. Immediately, there's an awkwardness that surrounded us — one that no one seemed to shake.

Chapter 4

The Razor's Eye

FEELING A BIT RATTLED, I HELD TIGHT TO the burlap sack on which I sat while the flames gave light to recapture our bearings. But something was amiss—I saw something move in the darkness from a corner of the room, making the strangest sounds. I could only see it in the shadows, unable to define who or what it was. All of the sudden, it jumped into the air and fluttered towards us, scratching and clawing as it took hold of the table, but I still can't see it.

The cloaked figure inched across the tabletop towards the candlelight where Brit was sitting. The next moment was one I know I'll always remember as my eyes began to pool. From out of the darkness it came, slowly strutting it's way closer and closer to the flame.

It was no spirit, no specter of the night… it was my best friend.

A strikingly handsome blue and gold macaw, brilliant in color and equally as wily.

"Hello Sam," blurted the highwayman Brit

with his nonchalant smile. Shotglass Sam—known by every living soul that has ever sailed under the black flag as a henchmen, confidant, and if you'll pardon the expression, 'wingman' to one of the most infamous pirates I've ever known... Barnacle Bill Bedlam, the Pirate King.

We had met some time ago in a place that I can't remember now, but I know I'll never forget, the tales we've told together —each one could write another book!

Sam took his place on the back of one of the two remaining empty chairs. The chair no doubt was meant for Barnacle Bill because wherever Sam is seen, his Master is never far behind... this I know.

I sat perfectly still, hoping to go unnoticed as my nervousness began to show. If he saw me, I'd most certainly be trapped.

Suddenly the last calm hair I had left on my head stood up as I noticed a small black scorpion slowly crawling across the bag on which I sit, moving towards my leg. The salty beads of saline from my forehead began to run into my eyes, burning, blinding. Still, I kept a watchful eye. I observed as it began its threatening decent up the hem of my trousers with a slow, domineering stride. I could feel every leg touch my skin as its crab-like walk became relentless torture.

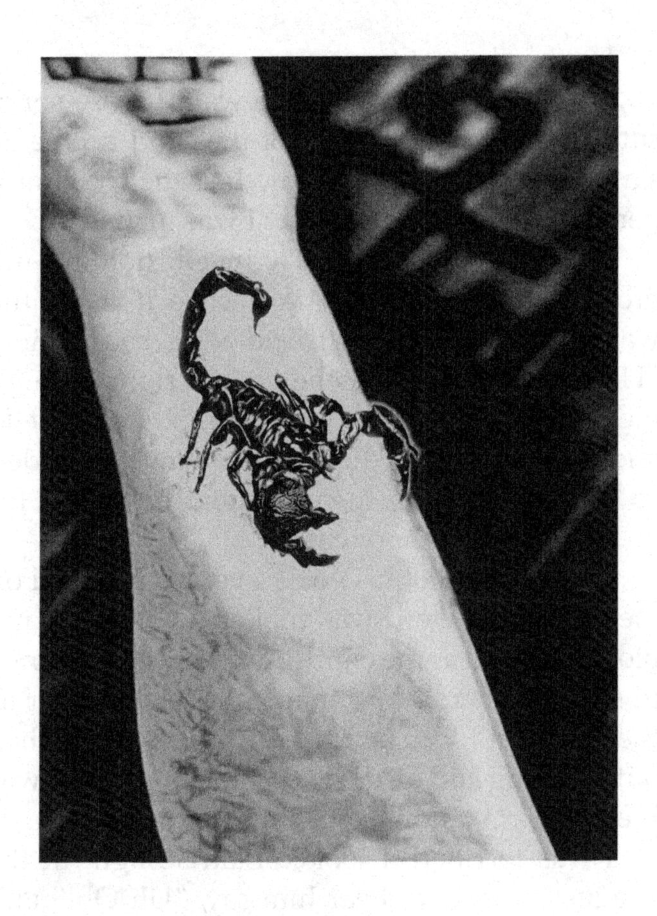

I watched 'til I could watch no more. In a nervous rant I snapped, swinging, kicking, and shaking like a leaf in a storm. No one seemed to pay me mind. They were too caught up drowning in their grog and insolent mutterings. Nary a salty scab bothered to even cut me an eye… none but one, Shotglass Sam. He pinned me in his sight the very instant that I drew back to swing at that venomous black bug.

He then knew.

With my back against the wall, I froze solid, sitting there on my throne of pins and needles. I saw his eyes dilate upon me like the focus of a periscope. It was then I knew I was made.

With eyes wide shut I cringed, holding my breathe as if it were my last. Then it came, the warm voice of an old friend with bad timing. "Hellaye," said Sam as he looked right through me. "Hellaye" is Sam's word. A mixture of Hello and Hi. He slurred the words often. It sounded so piratey that the men frequently used it for greetings, salutes and toasts.

At the sound of his voice, every eye turned on me though no word was spoken. I could feel my blood run cold as the entire krewe stared me down in silence. Then the strange got even stranger as the wall that I lean against began to push in then out, inhaling and exhaling as if the ship's wall was breathing... breathing at the base of my spine.

I was terrified. I looked Sam straight in the eye just in time to hear him say, "Uh Oh!" and then it came.

The wall I leaned up against exploded with the force of a musket blast blowing a hole two feet wide right beside my head. I thought to run but had no chance, something had a hold on me, pinning me down. I wondered if a shard of wood had snagged the collar of my shirt but to my misfortune that was not the case.

My obstruction was larger and much more menacing... it was Morgan. He had felt my presence even through the walls of his own ship. The horrific attack was not that of a musket's fire but one of sheer brute force. In his battle with aggression Morgan had punched a hole in the wall behind with his brass hand to catch me on his hook like a sea trout on the end of a fisherman's pole. I begin to flail about like a wet dog—a sad attempt to break free from his clutch, to no avail. I was stuck, I couldn't move my head.

From the corner of my eye I saw the very sharp and shiny brass hook at the hand of a bloodthirsty pirate. And it wasn't the collar of my shirt that he had snagged… it was me. With a razor's eye, the sharp point of his hook had pierced the lobe of my left ear and into the wood behind it leaving me still, backbone locked in fright. The funny thing is, I felt no pain as the ear was as numb as the rest of my body!

I could hear him laugh from beyond the wall as he cruelly turned the hook in my ear ever so slightly. Bound by a pirate's hook, imprisoned in this fearful moment, I was feeling like a Christian in a cage of lions as the slow cool drip of my arctic blood trickled down the nape of my neck.

"Hook," came a voice from across the room. "Stop buggering with the young prospect and take seat! The trials that command us are far more vital and require a clever eye!" It was a voice I had hoped to hear, a voice that had graced my memory.

It was he, The Pirate King, Barnacle Bill Bedlam that suddenly appeared from the shadows.

I could hear the wood squeak as Morgan slowly

pulled his hook from the wall freeing my bloody ear then entered the room with assertiveness and poise. He sauntered past, keeping his left eye on me at all times. I feared his judgment with me was not over as I begin to feel the pain.

The two men assumed their places at the round table and the Brethren Court was now complete, united as one, forged, and ready to pass judgment on the expedition into the unknown.

With a hearty "Hellaye," the ring of thieves are all called to order. They raise their glasses in honor and friendship—to good fortune, the code, the krewe, and their creed. "Hellaye!"

The Barnacle stood to speak. "A lesson learned in time, we cannot recover what was lost in the wake but tomorrow is ours to win or lose! They've found us again gents, the krewe of the *Neptune*. Their shadows speak out, they follow our every move," said the Barnacle with a sigh of disgust. "It would seem the sovereignty of Captain Charles Vane still plagues the world in which we live and the air we breathe... stealing our sailors in the night. We all knew this day would come. We must face our fears, take back what is rightfully ours... our lives!," growls Barnacle Bill with a low gruff voice.

I sat silent as the grave while the meeting of the minds pushed on, listening intently as the Legend of Carbonados was revealed, told before me in black and white. I hung on every word as if my life depended on it... because it did!

In truths and lies, as the story goes.

Barnacle Bill Bedlam, Bloody Bob Carver, Morgan the Hook, and various integral members of the BOC once served aboard the *Neptune* under the guidance of Captain Charles Vane. That was in their younger days when poaching fishing boats was all they were known for. From Cuba to the West Indies they plundered small vessels and merchant ships, barely making enough profit to keep afloat.

Another member of *Neptune's* krewe at that time was a young upstart of a pirate named John Rackham, affectionately known as Calico Jack. Jack never thought too much of Charles Vane's authority and was in constant turmoil as a result. He had heard through the grapevine that a longtime friend of Captain Vane's, named Lester Banks, would be taking sail soon. Among many things Lester was the son of a powerfully wealthy Spanish Conquistador by the name of Carbonados, who owned diamond mines in Latin America somewhere near Belize. He was a dark horse—always on the lamb. He was the Medicine Man they say. He practiced holistic medicine but I hear tell it was really Voodoo. A cultish figure, he has gone by many names over the years, Dolche, Malum, which I believe is Latin for evil, and the ever popular Wicked Lester.

With the arm of the law closing in, Lester had plans to move his practices, his wealth, and fortunes across the Caribbean to Guadeloupe where he planned to enlist the help of Captain Vane. That's when the mutiny began.

Calico Jack had put together a small alliance, a secret band of men known as his Skeleton Krewe, handpicked for their bravery and notoriety. These men were to take the ships belonging to Lester Banks, his wealth, his fortune, and his command. Much to his dismay Barnacle Bill and his mates were on that list regardless of choice. Young Barnacle Bill never really held Charles Vane in high regards. At times, he found Vane ruthless and cruel but he had no quarrels with the captain and certainly had no intentions of looting his friend's prosperity whether they be pirates or not. Barnacle was unaware of Rackham's intentions and chose to merely bide the chain of command. It was then that he planned his departure from the *Neptune.*

Barnacle, Bloody Bob, Morgan, and several others had heard of a number of Spanish Galleons that had sunk off the coast of Cuba near Cayo Largo, each containing over twenty four million in treasures. The pirates had set their sites on those seas and later, those very same men would form a brotherhood of pirates, the Union of Souls, known by many as the BOC, The Brethren of Caroline. But as it were, Calico Jack was second in command and when you're at sea, you "let *no* man break the chain!"

Chapter 5

The Legend of Carbonados

THE STAGE WAS SET AND THE MANDATE OF the Skeleton Krewe was subsequently carried out in a hale of cannon fire somewhere off the Dominican Republic on the coast of Mona Island. By the hand of Calico Jack, Charles Vane was abandoned on an island near Silver Shoal and left to rot.

The attack came with might and vigor. A superior show of light and smoke powdered the sky almost in rhythm, I'm told. One by one the ships were hit. The reef there was nearly a mile deep. Badly damaged, the ship's wealth, fortunes, and the krewe were lost to the depths. Nothing ventured… nothing gained.

There's no written truth that Lester Banks was ever aboard any of the vessels but speculation and the *legends and lies* live on. A specter of the sea, neither living nor dead some tell.

From the dark recesses of his mind came the spiritualistic conjuring of unearthly and unexplainable powers. They say he commanded the dead… "Equipo de los Muertos," which meant, Krewe of the Dead! The remains of the men that perished aboard his vessels still roam the seas in search of the Skeleton Krewe.

Many an ill-fated story has surfaced over the coarse of time that involved the men of the *Neptune* telling of strange occurrences, torrid tales of bizarre sightings, nocturnal visits of the damned—enough dread to shake the wake in the boldest of sailor. Each man bears the cross, his own bucket list of nightmares… including Bill Bedlam.

Some have perished from the Sword of Damocles. Some vanish without a trace never to be seen or heard from again. Others fall asleep in a pool of sweat waiting and wondering 'when will the bell toll for thee… when will they come for me?'.

The Barnacle refers to these evil apparitions as Tommyknockers—a word my Grandfather used to say around All Hallows Eve to instill a chill in the vivid imagination of a naive young lad. Oh, the wraiths, phantoms, manifestations of the mind, and things that go bump in the night! As a boy I thought these were only fables, ghost stories or a vicarious release of fear—not so, sorry to say. They dwell in our world and walk among us, watching us from the corners of their eyes, waiting to heed the demands of wicked Lester Banks.

The Barnacle droned on with the fiendish folklore and warnings as the meeting melted down like the candle. You could almost see a cloud of doom and despair heavily hang above their heads as they sat waiting for the last breath.

"Carpe diem," Barnacle Bill blurts out in the silence. With a puzzled eye, the court looks on in confusion. Suddenly, Bloody Bob warms up the table with his crooked smile—a look as if he'd finally solved the joke that had no answer. Carpe diem or *seize the day,* aside from the irony that it bestowed in that company, was a phrase used in frequency by a voice gone by. It was the voice of a dysfunctional member of youth.

Have you ever had a friend that you loved to hate? The one with all the right answers, the fancy dress, the one that sneers at you with an "I told ya so?" In this company, his name was Cygnus. The square peg, the one that didn't quite fit.

His estranged mannerisms had led him to a life of seclusion. He showed autistic talents with a mind of vast knowledge. The lad remembered every word from every book, every verse from every song… every moment in time! But he shielded himself from the public and would answer only at random. It could be said that he kept a protective bubble around himself—a bubble filled with loneliness.

With a text book brain and the social skills of an infant, he locked away the world as if it meant to do him harm.

Barnacle Bill Bedlam and Bloody Bob Carver, however were just the opposite—precocious and meddlesome. So curious of life and it's treasures, they wore those black streaks down their back with pride.

The boys knew their friend had made it his life's work to study the world's cultures and religions. They also knew that the beacon that would save their souls lay deep in Caribbean waters.

The Haitians had a sacrament or rite, one known to free a man of his demons, free him of his sins. They possessed a totem, an amulet or talisman capable of worldly powers of sovereignty and grace. Known as "Kuma-wani," the Spirit of the Sea or Sea Spirit to the Haitians, it was a demigod—a symbol of purity and faith, figure of spirituality, of emancipation and deliverance. But to the men of the Skeleton Krewe, it was their only hope. Their one shot at salvation from a life of peril and purgatory. They had to take it. They had no choice!

"We must find Cygnus," spouted the jaded Bill Bedlam. "We must find the spirit to survive! We'll chart a coarse for Pavo Realle… our fate lies with Swan."

The gathering had settled and all revealed of the Legend of Carbonados. This wasn't to be a voyage of prosperity or pride, no treasures of the deep lie awaiting these men, no gold at the end of their rainbow. This was a voyage of survival, a fight to exist and to live on. Theirs was a quest for humanity, to save their mortal souls from a fate never wanted. It was a corner they had been painted into.

In that melancholy moment, I sat and watched in

tragic observance the hands of Bill Bedlam, feeling his torment with him. The one person that I hold in regard as the pirate of all pirates looked weary, chilled to the marrow, a victim of circumstance.

As they gathered themselves up to leave, I could feel the eyes of Morgan the Hook upon me. I turned to look but he wasn't there. I turned back in haste with plans to head for the door, fumbling and bumping my head into the butt of a gun… a pistol mounted on the chest of Morgan the Hook. He was a mountain of a man, so much taller than I, and all I could do was to just stand there and stare at the gun, much too afraid to look up.

"Are ye lost boy?"

I could feel the warm resonance of his voice breathing down upon me as he spoke.

"A wrong turn in time perhaps!"

He looked down in anger then rested his hand upon his pistol's stock, fingers tapping on the barrel. I stood in perfect form with eyes squinting as I awaited the worst of it.

With his right hand, he slowly peeled a silver hoop earring from his ear then dipped it in a whiskey glass that sat at the table by his side. With rather large fingers, he fished the earring out of the booze and threw it onto the table right in front of me. I simply looked at the earring not knowing how to respond. "Best not let that hole close up boy!" he said.

I stared at him, incredulous at what he'd said. Could it be true that he offered me a token? Without pause, I took the earring in my hand and stared at it dumbfounded. As he began to walk away, I remembered his last words, 'Take the ring boy. If ever I find you squandering aboard my ship again, I'll open a hole in your head much larger. Savvy?"

Then by those words, he was gone. Painfully I speared the hoop through my bloody lobe... and I still wear it to this day!

The true blood of a pirate is evanescent, fleeting, like everything else on God's green orb. It's never meant to last. The day will come when there will be none left at all, just a memory, a recollection, a page in a book, as will I.

Truth be known, as the sands of time blow past me, I wage my wars with the man in the mirror too, even at the ripe old age of fifteen. Living in denial is a crime of conscience—futile and trite. The black mark drawn upon my ancestors is the same mark that I bear, the mark of a pirate. There's the truth of it!

With a fire down below and not a second to burn, I was on the move. Still unsure of my role on this ghoulish, trek I bound my way to the ship's surface hoping the stars would steer me to safety before that deadly whip of fate could come down upon me.

With a fool's brass and a moments pass, all hope had gone. The one glimmer of promise I had left to cling to had failed me. Feeling a bit seasick I stood alone on deck in a cloud of darkness. I could see nothing—no land, no stars, no horizon. Somewhere in the night, somewhere in my fits of despair, we had quietly slipped away and I was once again lost to wander this world with no notion of what I'd done, where I was, or how I would get back home.

The beast of burden now owned me. As the ship sailed on into the night, I had no say. Merely along for the ride, for whatever sufferings this voyage has in store, was I. The flicker of candlelight towards the ships aft beckoned me, so I followed it. With a snakes slither, I slowly made my approach, feeling my way through the darkness. I turned a corner on this dreadful evening to find none other than my smile, for under the candlelight, perched on the rail of the ship was my old feathered friend Shotglass Sam. This was a very comforting moment for me, I would say. It was like he was there to await my arrival, like so many times before.

His eyes took to me then he blinked and stretched out his lower jaw, almost as if he were trying to smile. Then it came, the infamous "Hellaye!" – the call that he is best noted for.

"Hellaye," I replied softly.

"Whatcha doin?" he said.

"I'm afraid I'm lost and I can't find my way home," I said with a weak and weary voice.

He cocked his head to look at me with only one eye, like pirates do. I felt as if he knew I were tellin' tales! Suddenly, a voice from the past broke into the shadows behind me.

"Careful Mr. Bones. Lies run deep as the ocean blue. If you're not wary, they can consume you!"

I turned my back and there he stood beneath

the candlelight, hiding behind a crooked smile and chewing on a corn cob pipe. It was the captain of the BOC, the one who saved my life a time or two, at least. He was the Crowned Prince of pirates—Barnacle Bill Bedlam, looking as coy as he could be.

"Were you lost when you trekked your way aboard this ship with that sack of feed bearin' ya down?" he asked, his voice slathered with distain. I hesitated to answer, wondering how he knew as I watched him as he smoked on a pipe that wasn't lit.

"Excuse me Sir but you can't smoke with no flame."

"I quit," he blurted. "Nasty habit really," he added as an afterthought.

"Then why the pipe?" I seemed to speak out of time.

"Bloody Bob gave this to me… a token of friendship," he said and stared at the pipe held out in his hand. A moment later, he put it back in his mouth, clinched tightly between his teeth, and displayed his crooked smile. Out of respect, I spoke no more of the corn cob pipe.

Chapter 6

Rainbow on my World

"IF YOU'RE LOOKING FOR THE DOORWAY that leads you home, I can't help you." He paused then added, "I'm afraid you're a bit too late." He could see I was a troublesome young lad and boyishly jokes to get my appeal. "We've found our heading," he said, another joke. Finally, when he could see that it wasn't working, he lowered his gaze and said, "Walk with me Mr. Bones."

We made our way towards the fore or front of the ship at a normal pace. Immediately, I started in on him with my bag of stupid questions. He pings back with an occasional, "Uh huh," blatantly ignoring me as he continued to look over his left shoulder at the sea. His pace suddenly increased and I found it difficult to keep up.

"Our time is at hand boy!" he barked loudly as we broke out into a run. "Spell me yon Mr. Bones," he says. "Have you ever seen an Indian summer in Pavo Realle?"

Just then, out through the clouds off of the port

side comes a magnificent ship! It moved along side of us, not close enough to touch but hard enough to see in the night. She was a few tics faster too. A chill came over me. I knew the ship—I'd walked aboard her.

"The mother ship, *Calypso's Revenge,*" I breathed.

With our tails in the wind, Barnacle sprang off of a rum crate into the night sky, obviously hoping to time his jump with the passing ship. He swung out to her, grabbing onto the rope net that hung from her starboard. Clinging to the net like a crab, I could hear him shout "Bones! Move it along and hurry!"

I was two steps behind and moving fast with my mind racing: *should I stay or jump?* She kept quite a pace that left no time for options. So I leapt from the same rum crate and reached out a hand for a sail's rope… that wasn't there. I started to flail my arms in panic as I fell through the air. With one hand, I managed to grab hold of the last rung from the rope ladder as the ship sailed by. With all my strength, I gripped to her tightly while my body dangled, waves crashing against my feet in an attempt to draw me under.

With every bit of fight I had in me, I pulled myself up and up until finally falling aboard the *Revenge* like a prize fish, flopping and shaking, landing in the arms of the one called Boo.

To say the least, I felt a bit tattered and worn but I managed to peel an eye. There she was, smiling… jeering… staring at me with eyes as brown as the trunk on a whispering pine.

Isn't it funny how certain moments in time, a glance, a remembrance, can have such a calming effect over you? A sweet fragrance, a feeling of home… this was that moment! I could see the sunlight through her eyes as I laid there, playing up the helpless rescue a wee bit much just to get her attention—to dote on me and to hold me for just a bit longer.

Her name is Savannah Faith but she known in folklore as just Boo. The daughter of those notorious pirates, Barnacle Bill and Scarlett DeVille. Now, one might think that being the child of infamous pirates would make her rebellious and crude. Quite the contrary, you see… I know her. She is joyful and kind with a heart filled with hope. Her hair smells like jasmine if you stand too close and 'when she smiles, God smiles with her then gently paints a rainbow on my world!' Those familiar words are used by the Barnacle whenever he swoons over his beloved child and I must confess, I stole that line from him.

With warm intentions, she struggled desperately to get me to my feet, tugging on my arm like a workhorse, but I had not a leg left to stand on. The events of the day had bled me… literally.

I laid there as lifeless as a sea slug, with nothing to show for it but a blood stained shirt and one shoe lost at sea. Still, I was in the arms of goodness… this I knew! She was someone I could trust. Slowly, I felt my fire fizzle, my mind and body began to let go. The last thing I remembered as I faded from consciousness in the arms of a friend, was hearing the voice of Shotglass Sam so poetically say, "Goodnight."

And thus my day was done.

*****

A new day rose as I awoke in a sea of wonderment, which I sometimes do, still shaking off the cobwebs from an exasperating day before. From the moment I opened my eyes, I saw a promise of brighter days ahead. Things were looking up as I laid there literally *looking up* into blue skies and blue eyes that stared back at me. It seemed that I had fallen into the good care of pirate royalty.

Lady Scarlett DeVille smiled down at me. She held a cup of tea as she moved to block the sunlight from my eyes just long enough to see her. The sunburst created a surreal divine glow around her—an aura, as it were. Her long blonde hair shined, framing her face as I slowly daydreamed in aqua marine. I've said it in times 'o plenty, 'Bill Bedlam chose his lady well'. With a subtle smile, I ponder, *may I one day be this blessed!*

"Still chasing after tomorrow, today? Is that it young Tyler?" said Lady Scarlett as she and Boo watch over me. Sitting up, I take the cup from her hand and nod gratefully as I take a sip.

"No one has used my proper name in a long while," I replied.

Right then she stopped smiling. "If it's a treasure hunt filled with dreams and schemes you're seeking, I'm afraid you've been misinformed!" The comment was clearly a warning from the bride of Barnacle Bill Bedlam. "This is a sail of a different coarse," she added. "One of jeopardy and risk! These evils need not have concerned you… but now they know your name! The moment you took sail aboard this vessel, you chose a side. You chose a destiny in a world you know nothing of. You remain part of the Krewe without choice, without reason!" Her eyes locked onto me as Lady Scarlett spoke bluntly and straight faced. Just then we both heard footsteps of someone approaching. "Pray for rain when the darkness comes," she said. The comment knocked me off coarse… I didn't understand her meaning. "They'll be looking for you too," she added, another dagger spoken in a different tone that reaffirmed my doubts and fears.

One soggy looking sod from the Krewe peered from the door. "Mr. Bones to see the Captain," he said rather gruffly.

I rose to my feet to follow the gent when suddenly Savannah shouted loudly and emphatic, surely to get my attention, "BONES!"

I paused, looking back with an open mind and open heart. Boo then stomped her foot, crossed her arms, and scowled at her mother as if to get her to do something. Even in my fearful position, I had to hold my breath so as not to snicker… it was the sweetest thing!

Scarlett DeVille then spoke words so profound, it stirred my very soul. "A wise old bird once told me," said she. "If the tempest of your journey is bearing down on you., days and nights seem endless and torrent. Do me a favor…"

"What's that?" I asked with my naiveté and half a smile.

She leaned forward and breathed her reply, "Learn how to dance in the rain!" These words I will always remember.

With a pit in my throat and a heart redeemed, I turned away and with a smile, I was gone.

The distance was short but the walk seemed to last forever as I made may way upon the path to see the pirate king. I know naught of what lies ahead—could it be the Barnacle's wrath or an impending fate of the dark prophecy awaiting us all.

I arrive to find Bill Bedlam in a state of anguish, wrestling at the wheel of the *Revenge,* gnashing his teeth. "Down two sheets and held fast," he shouts. Of course, I knew it meant lower two sails to scrub off speed. All eyes beamed out to a strange black spot on the horizon. Now it was a right clear day with the sun shining from the heavens and the crystal Caribbean waters so pure, you could see to the bottom. So what was it that lay beneath the surface directly in the path of our ship?

The more we drew near, the larger the dark cell grew. It must have been a hundred yards wide or more, twice as long in depth. Minutes passed. Soon we were upon it. It crested beneath us and all around the ship that was surrounded in black water. As we moved, the dark water moved with us. What ever it was, we seemed to have attracted it. Imagine my delight; *was Jonah once again ringing in my ear?*

"Keep a steady pace and a sharp eye, I certainly mean them no harm," commanded the captain as he began to… smile?

Oh bullock! I know that look, I've seen that smile before. That's the smile that makes me cringe in suspicion, that very same smile made me believe that the other shoe was about to drop!

But before my eyes, to my shock and surprise, I couldn't have been more wrong. What I was to witness just seconds later would change me. It was by far the biggest spectacle of beauty and grace that God had ever chosen to share with a boy like me.

It was truly a day to remember.

At that moment I heard Barnacle let go a laugh—a laugh from the deepest part of his belly just as the dark cell surfaced. I watched the black water turn to whitecap as hundreds upon hundreds of pink belly dolphins took to the air around us. Wide eyed and bushy-tailed, I clung to the rail of the ship lost in amazement.

Up and down, in and out, piercing the water with precision and speed, they ran together in perfect harmony sewing their way across the sea. It was a stampede of dolphins, the largest pod I had ever seen. There must have been a thousand or more, franticly swimming to keep up with the ship or perhaps just to race the wind.

As I stood, leering and breathless in awe,

something began to trouble me. One thought weighed on my mind. I want so badly to revel in this miraculous moment but I couldn't because no matter how much this marvel had moved me, I knew a certain someone who would love it just a little bit more. It hit me that I must find Boo… and fast!

I turned back for the cabin to fetch her and there she was, standing right by my side. There was no telling how long she had been there. Her eyes were opened just as wide, tail just as bushy!

I tugged her hand and off we went, laughing, smiling, and bouncing from one end of the ship to the other as we watched this wonder take place.

She must have named every single dolphin as we took it in together.

It was a special moment in time, one I'll surely relish. I must say that at the wee age of fifteen, I've surely grown a rusty old heart… but I've always meant well.

Chapter 7

The Looking Glass

THE POD TOYED WITH US UNTIL THEY HAD their fill—we then parted ways. They veered southeast towards Barbados as we stayed on course due south in search of Pavo Realle—a small isle of very few inhabitants, deep in Caribbean waters near Old Providence Island, from what I was told. It was there that we would find the key to unlock the Pandora's box that held our very souls.

We ran in the heat, headed for the stairwell that led to the quarterdeck for one last glimpse of the stampede as they faded from sight, when I started to make mistakes.

Instantly, those feelings came again...

An over excitable boy at times I guess—I zigged when I should've zagged. I stumbled on the top step and fell face forward into a netted pile of fish that had been caught for the evening's dinner. Covered in their salty stench, I listened to Savannah laugh nearly to the brink of tears as I stared down the mouth of a large sea bass. A few tics later, I was back on my feet, dusting off the chum and certainly being humbled while Boo fought to regain composure. She let go of the laughter and bliss for a moment but kept her sweet sincere smile as she tried her best not to make me feel any more foolish. But it happened just the same!

No sooner than I shrugged off the incident and looked Boo in the eyes than she began to wave joyfully… and that's when the other shoe dropped!

Like a fool I begin to wave back, like some sort of affliction had hit me. In fact, it wasn't me she was waving to at all. A cold chill of sea spray blew in off the sea and right up my spine. Savannah then snares her best Cheshire-grin and said, "Hello Daddy."

I looked to the deck just in time to see a rather large, shadowy figure rise from behind. I could feel the wooden planks beneath my feet give, as if someone were standing right behind me, but like a coward, I didn't have the *"Barnacles"* to turn around. Instead, I just closed my eyes.

Raspy and bold words rang over my shoulder. "Well… if it isn't the unfortunate son. You had the world to live for and you blew it the moment we cast away."

I turned slowly to look him in the eye. It was Barnacle Bill Bedlam. As he stared me down, he said these words. "Dire are the days when a man trades his soul for another. You know not what you've done boy—tangled in a web you'll never be free from. Indeed, these ill gotten games of vanity and greed will bury you."

I stared at him, unsure how to respond and he continued.

"This is not a mission of fortune, no sunset cruise. Your days of being are numbered, marked for death, your very life now lies in the hands of a wicked Baron as he watches you through his looking glass, measuring your hopes and dreams. There's no escape, boy. The world you once knew is gone."

Barnacle looked down at a gold compass

clenched tightly in his fist then glanced far out onto the horizon. As long as I have known him, I've never seen an expression of doubt cross his face, never that look of uncertainty… until now. It was then that I faced the whole truth of it—this was to be a one way trip. We weren't coming back.

With a pit in my stomach, and feeling downhearted, I silently festered in denial, wishing I 'didn't know now what I didn't know then'.

Suddenly, the Barnacle growled out, "Dark days ahead Mr. Bones. Ya best pray with all your might! We have but one chance to save us from this curse, one chance to survive!"

I heard the ship's bell ring as we neared land, the first stop on this voyage of despair. We were somewhere off the coast of Jamaica at a small Island known as Te Amare. The Barnacle tells me it's Spanish, short for the phrase, 'Te amare por siempre', which means 'I'll love you forever'.

Legend states that the island gained its name from the infamous pirate Captain William Kidd. As the story goes, Captain Kidd had fallen in love with a beauty from Costa Rica and they were secretly betrothed. She was new to the Island—brought there to be by his side. Not long thereafter she became ill, rheumatic fever they say. She passed one morning in her sleep. William awoke to find her head peacefully resting on his shoulder, her hand wrapped tightly in his palm. She was put to rest on the Island near Barbary Cove. He named the Island Te Amare in homage to a love lost then he sailed out of sight never to return.

But I digress, we were there for one reason and one reason only... to find a pirate... a member of the BOC. Soon, we were informed of her whereabouts.

You see, Bill Bedlam knew of Pavo Realle but he did not know its exact location. Our brethren were our guide, those that were familiar with these waters though it wouldn't be easy. I heard tell that the island's mystery and intrigue date back to long before my time. There was a small Swahili tribe far from Kenya who dwelt in the north woods. These people believed that on the night of the crescent moon, the island could move with the sea. Indeed, the island was a place of many secrets and that was the attraction that brought Cygnus to Pavo Realle. He wanted seclusion—he wanted a place where he would never be found.

The man that we were in search of, the one that would serve as the ship's navigator and guide us to the perplexing Island of Pavo Realle, is known only by one name... Hawkeye.

Never has there been any account written of her given name, neither was it ever spoken. From what I gathered, she was barely my height but still stood tall, was brass and bold to whatever came her way. She had what the Barnacle referred to as "Alligator Etiquette," creating a charming facade by her entrancing, sinful stare and crossword smile, all the while slithering up behind a man to size him up for conquest or conquer.

She was the essence of a true pirate.

Hawkeye came to prospect with the Brethren

of Caroline after a near miss with the gallows. Falsely accused of impersonating a Pontiff before King and Court and while preceding over three christenings for the Queen, she passed judgment in a court that changed the laws of religious persecution for woman in the early 19th-century—but not before she made off with the tides of gold left for the christenings. She even took the sacrificial wine. Hawkeye made a safe escape but was apprehended days later in a pub down on the waterfront in Bexley. They found her dressed in white, dancing to *Spanish Ladies* in full Bishop regalia… pointy hat and all! The alabaster robe was slightly stained scarlet red from the bottle of sacrificial wine she had clenched in her hand. The woman loved to dance!

"Your life is a chalice, you must fill it! Learn to laugh at yourself," she would say to those she met.

Bloody Bob and Barnacle sprung her from a London cell two days before she was to meet the hangman's noose.

"She's a wonderful resource of *assertive fortitude,* as I like to call it—the power of invention. A good pirate!" Barnacle Bill would swear by it. "You see Mr. Bones, without imagination you have naught, no reasons no rhymes. Imagination holds more value than knowledge or power! Knowledge is an illusion of a narrow mind, power is fleeting… never meant to last, but with imagination you can live on forever, with imagination you can be free!"

We made our arrival off the coast of Te Amare and none too soon, as we immediately saw the coats a-comin'! From my vantage point, or lack of it, I could clearly see two Navy ships—the *Dreadnought* and *Britannia.* The *Britannia* sat silent and still fifty yards off shore while the larger ship, the *Dreadnought* was two hundred yards out and approaching.

We were not a far cry from the southern most point of Jamaica, not a far cry from Port Royal. We would sail within their grasp, their stronghold. They may have had wind of our arrival, they may well have been watching us! Sadly, we did not know. The Island was a sweet spot for Royal Fleet scruds to earn their colors, their rank, their license to kill all of those accused of piracy.

Only a two day sail from the shores of Jamaica, this place hosted the company's brazen brass come here to flex their wings and exploit the strength of their pompous regime. Funny, for an island that was given its name from a love lost… I could see no love lost there!

The Barnacle reappeared, tall at the wheel and smiling into the sun, boasting his commands with valor and charm. "We'll anchor down on the isle's west side by Barbary Cove. They'll be none the wiser!"

With a swift and stylish slide of his hand, Barnacle scooped Sam up to place him on his shoulder. He then pulled a peanut from his pocket and primed his feathered friend. He looked to the bird and with a task on his tongue said, "Find Hawkeye. Tell her I'll be waiting… the usual place."

Sam took flight, never looking back. I watched as he soared high in a sunset sky and disappeared into the dusk. Captain and Krewe prepared to go ashore... but where? We anchored near a canal but all I could see was a swamp with marshlands tall in the thicket.

"Lower the longboat," called out the captain.

As I waited my turn to board the small craft, I was unable to secure the same boat as Captain Barnacle. It had already been filled with men so I joined the Krewe on boat number two.

I heard the Barnacle call out to me as we begin to push off, "Mr. Bones! Keep yer wits about ya boy. Stay with the Krewe! I know not what the night will bring!"

Oh bugger! A warm welcome to the island no less. His fair warning bred paranoia, this I knew. As we began spooning our way upstream, I heard him belt his final advisory and these words stayed with me throughout the entire journey. He said, "Watch out for the Tommyknockers!"

The night closed in. The harmonizing sounds of the bullfrogs and the crickets was almost deafening as our two small boats slowly drifted into the darkness. I watched the fireflies dance in the light and caught sight of the gators hidden in the reeds, leering at us with hungry eyes as we gently passed. Deeper into the woods we forged on with not a word spoken. Blanketed by a dark night we came upon a place bled with moonbeams. The vivid light shined down just like rain to cast an eerie glow on this small cove in the middle of nowhere. I caught a glimpse of a small, crudely made sign, cross shaped and hammered into the sand by the shoreline. It read *Barbary Cove*.

Call me crazy, but it was no sooner that we rowed passed the marker to enter the revered burial grounds of the notable William Kidd's mistress than I started to hear voices.

Chapter 8

Skullduggery

JUST BEYOND THE WATERS EDGE, HIDDEN in the trees, a flicker of light caught my eye. Its reflection danced like a gypsy flame. The longer I stared at it, the brighter the ghostly light became, holding my attention in chains. It seemed to be a daydream at night.

I compelled myself to turn away from it to break the trance. With sunspots in my eyes, I saw a man stand by the bay, partially hidden in the palms. He was a shell of a man, wrinkled and pale, grey in color, and dressed in pirate's clothing. He watched me with angry eyes as I stared back in fear. Then it came… the first whisper.

As the games of Skullduggery began, the voice came from behind my left ear. If that doesn't scare you then hear this, the words were so close I could feel his breath on the back of my neck! The voice said clearly, "Sin piedad."

Cast voices – it was the voice of the stranger on the riverbank, but how? I watched his lips move as I felt the evil whisper come from behind. I spun around, shivering, but no one was there.

Quickly, spinning on my heels, I turned back to find the man in the pindo palms but he was gone. Tommyknockers—they move in the darkness.

"Sin piedad." I knew not what it meant so I did what I do best… I badgered the Barnacle for answers as he sat in the boat. All the same, I should've kept my big mouth shut!

He wasn't hesitant to share as he looked me in the eyes. "No mercy," he said. "Sin piedad means no mercy." The silence of the reality consumed me. We didn't speak again until the boats were set ashore.

The exotic light that captivated my attention came from an old wooden shack in the woods that rested on an inlet. Quite small, it had sort of a native tribal appeal to it. Bamboo walls, palm thatch roof, snakes in the trees, and creatures of the wild abundance -- the island's only answer to a speak-easy or tavern. It seemed peculiar how the Barnacle and his Krewe always seem to sniff out ale houses even in the middle of a jungle? I thought I could see a pattern develop there.

They called the place *La Palabra,* it meant The Skippers—a tavern in the front and a smokehouse in the back, all on the water. We were here to meet Hawkeye there, tell her of our intentions, and take sail. It was a plan to cut 'n dry.

From my eye, I could see no signs of the company—no colors flying. I prayed we would be in and out with haste!

We rattled and clunked our way through the door like a sacred cow, only to find Hawkeye and

Shotglass Sam awaiting. We must have brought an intimidating aura with us because the locals all seemed to shy away as we took seat at the table where Hawkeye sat. The murmuring soon began.

Loosely decorated in nautical equipment and scrap, the place was filled with mostly junk from old ships no one wanted, although one item caught my eye. It stood out from all the rest -- a cannon, small in size and mounted to a pedestal on the bar. It was only about as long as my arm and was a swivel gun, I was told. As I went in for a closer look, I noticed an inscription just below the belly of the weapon. A small plaque was mounted to the base of the pedestal and handwritten on it read, "Buckboard Betty." It would seem that our thunderous friend had been given a name. The thing was quite a beautiful piece of artillery. I wondered if it fired?

Barnacle and Bloody Bob begin to enthrall Hawkeye with words she didn't want to hear on a day she didn't want to come with us. She hadn't an option you see, the clock ticked for her too! As a standing member of the BOC, she too bore the curse of Wicked Lester and his "Equipo de los Muertos."

As the two pirates continued to deliver their grim ultimatums to Hawkeye, I was distracted by the aromas floating from the smokehouse. I left my place at the table just for a moment to follow my stomach. The gent was cooking up a mess of Boudin or Boodang, as it was called on the island. With a slight of hand, I snaked a hard roll, some Boodang, and quickly made myself scarce. With an empty belly and blatant lack of manners, I gorged myself as I trudged back to the table. Upon my return I found my place and seat was not as I had left it. A flower lay on the table and strange words had been carved into the tabletop at the very spot that I had been sitting. No one had moved from the table around me, yet it seems that no one saw a thing. The scribe read, *nos la olvidamos nos muestran sin piedad.*

Puzzled and somewhat gun-shy, I took the flower in my hand, and within a breath I watched the flower wilt then die, right before my very eyes. Quickly, I wrangled the Barnacle for my delusional show and tell. With one look he knew. His face showed no emotion and you could barely hear his voice as he muttered the word, "Dragon."

Apparently, the flower I held was called a 'Snapdragon'. Throughout its life, it was a beautiful flower but when it began to wilt and die, it took on a rather macabre shape… the shape of a human skull. That was the calling card of Lester Banks, so I'm told.

Cryptic in warning, those words carved into the table: *Nos la olvidamos nos muestran sin piedad,* which meant, 'We are the forsaken, we show no mercy'. It seems they knew where to find me – the Krewe of Los Muertos. I had nowhere to hide, I was marked with the Black Spot. Alarmed by the impending vendetta while holding a fist full of snapdragon skulls, we all agreed it was time to go!

As long as I'd known Barnacle Bill Bedlam, rarely had he ever left a place the same way as he'd found it. This time was no exception.

As the crow flies, it didn't take long before a number of tavern murmurs had reached the Naval ship *Britannia* docked just off shore. With Hawkeye's head still swimming in despondence, we took her by the wrist and began our migration towards the exit, leaving nothing to chance. The closer we drew to the door, the closer we drew to our pistols!

There were no windows to spy through so we had to "see" with our ears. The night's humming fell silent. "Can you hear it?" sparked Bloody Bob Carver. I heard nothing… nothing but the unnerving silence of the great outdoors.

Oddly enough, you would think that being the only watering hole on this Island, there would be more clamor, ruckus, general merriment, maybe even a brawl here or there but there was not a sound, not even the call of a bird or cricket. Bloody Bob had made his point loud and clear!

An ungodly smell of snakes filled the air, setting off the crisp steel sound of gun hammers being cocked in sequence all around me as we readied ourselves for a narrow escape. With fire in our hearts and armed in determination, we counted every breath as we idly waited for the opportune window… a time to flee.

Based on the trademark sounds and a pirate's cunning, we knew the infantry had arrived. I leaned in for a closer look when I heard Barnacle's call, "Stand Down Boy!" But I didn't budge. I was too desperate to hear who or what was there. In the same breath he finally belted out rather angrily, "Get… Out… Of… The… Way!"

The moments that followed were steadfast and quick. Just in the nick of time, I turned back to find Barnacle Bill Bedlam two steps behind me. He stood tall in a gunners stance, wild eyes gleaming with Buckboard Betty resting on his hip, barrel pointed straight at me!

I could see his crooked smile as my eyes grew wide as an owl's. I took it upon myself to *move* as I watched the fuse from my life fizzle away! Hysterically diving for the corner table, one thing played on my mind—the sole intention to kick my own butt for asking if the dang thing could fire!

Well it can.

As I landed in a pool of spilt grog and ashes, I barely had enough time to cover my ears before the blast did its damage. Take my word, Betty packs quite a punch! I watched it take out the entire wall, blown to splinters! The sound was deafening even with a covered ear.

The concussion from the cannon unmounted from its stand threw the Barnacle back against the wall. Kicked back with such force, the cannon tore a hole in the back wall, creating a hole big enough for us all to crawl through.

Barnacle came to his feet, looking a bit rattled and shaking his head. His eyes remained cloudy and a slightly swerving Barnacle choose this time to humor me with a quip! He looked me in the eye, sea legged and straight faced, and said, "I have a way with women!" Unbelievably, the man boasted of his whirlwind romance with a cannon affectionately named Buckboard Betty! And through the rabbit hole, *like {a} true pirates,* we vanished in the smoke and debris! There would be no telling what they would find when the dust settled.

We made our way to the riverbanks in true pirate fashion… cocked and loaded!

In the attempt to write us off the page, dead silence from the woods, screamed a warning. Held just seconds before and overcome with adrenaline that fueled revelry and gunplay, we blasted our way down to the shoreline loud and proud! The flintlock's fire lit the night as we took to the boats in a blaze.

After a flamboyant showing, we doused the lamps and shoved off to slink our way back to the ship, riding high on the moment but forever grateful that we were still breathing. As we wound down river with little time to ponder, I stared at the stars' reflections that floated atop the black water. Te Amare left quite a wake in my mind.

We got back to the mother ship and docked along side her. The Krewe climbed

aboard in turn as I stood in the boat awaiting mine. I briefly looked down to see something floating in the water near the surface. I began to feel a little uneasy as I stood there vulnerable, caught in a net. I kept feeding my head thoughts, *maybe it's just a hammerhead shark, they migrate to these Islands in the heat or perhaps a mermaid had come to share her salty kisses.*

I looked up in hope that the ladder would be free but it carried too many still. I'd have to wait a bit longer. I fearfully looked back to the black water only to witness a nightmare, a most horrific sight. I was terrified! In the depths beneath me, it was no shark… no mermaid.

A human hand shot straight out of the water beside me, bobbing up and down as if it were on springs. It looked grey and wrinkled from the sea, covered in kelp and barnacles. It's fingers were contracted, curved under like a monkeys paw. I had to shy away for fear, pinning it all on bad Boodang and lack of sleep!

Chapter 9

Neptune's Nest

MY BATTLE OF WILLS HAD PROVEN USELESS in the past. I was as spineless as the jellyfish when it came to temptation and my brain worked overtime to fool me into one more look back at such a gruesome discovery.

I had to look back, didn't I?

The hand floated on moonlight feeding into my torment. I leaned over the boat feeling nauseous and short of breath. As I did, the grizzly hand came alive, grabbed for me, and pulled me down! I gave it my all to resist the fiendish appendage but its hold was unwilling, deadly and cold... very cold.

As I was drawn over the edge, I could see a face just a few feet below the water's surface. It was too dark to see any detail but it was a face nonetheless, staring up at me from deep below.

I wrestled vigorously to break its grip. The more I fought the more angry it became. In a rage, the spectral head rose to the surface like the strike of an eel, coming straight for me! It gave a horrible, shrill scream—a banshee's cry. You could hear it echo from across the lagoon. It scared me so badly that I flinched and with all my might, pulled free from the cold clammy hand of the corpse. In so doing, I lost my balance and fell backward over the side of the boat, head first into the dark watery abyss.

As I tumbled my jaded memory placed the face and I cried out just before going under, "I know who you are!"

The chill of the cool night ocean upon my skin was no match to the bitter, frightful waters that I found myself submerged in. With eyes wide shut, I begin to tread for my life… but I wasn't moving and was losing air fast.

Frantic and foolish I peeled an eye. In the light of the dark waters I could see it there, holding me, shaking me like a rattle! I tried to scream, only to inhale salt water. It's eyes coiled open, lifeless and black, as it's lower jaw fell loosely to it's neck, appearing as if it were dislocated.

The last thing that I remembered was the feeling of hands on the back of my throat and the murky sound of death as it tried to take me. The jawless blue cadaver kept its hallow eyes upon me as it gurgled the words, "Sin piedad."

With a splash, the hands on the back of my neck took hold of my shirt collar and yanked me from the water into the longboat in one swift motion. It was Barnacle Bill. He had me by the neck as he hung from the main ships ladder. Still in shock, I sputtered and shook, drooling saltwater as I begged of the captain, "You must have seen it! You must have heard!"

"What are you rambling about Bones?" said Barnacle. "Your foolish desire for a midnight swim perhaps?"

"No sir," I replied. "It was Tommyknockers, Los Muertos. I've seen him before, I remember the face! It was the same spirit that marked me… the pirate hidden in the pindo palms from across the river!"

Barnacle Bill took a short pause and studied me. "I know not what you speak of boy. Your eyes look shot. Have you been in the rum?" he asked with a voice that was far too serene. He looked at me puzzled but not in disbelief.

"Certainly you heard the scream," I said. "Must've echoed for miles!"

"The only sound I recall was that of a daft young rube keying on my last nerve, drawing attention to my ship!" replied the Barnacle. "I watched as you lost the boat line in the water, you leaned over to fish it out, and got your sleeve caught on the oar rigging. You tugged and tore at your shirt like a fox with his foot in a trap before you finally fell backwards into the sea. Enough of the boyish immaturities. Now climb aboard. We must make Pavo Realle before the weather breaks!"

Impossible, I told myself. *He didn't see a thing… never heard a sound, but how?*

As I climbed the ladder to *Calypso's Revenge,* I spotted the cross sign of Barbary Cove once more—this time from a different view. At such a close distance, I saw that the back of the sign appeared to be marked. On a midnight watch as we bid farewell to Te Amare, we passed the crooked old sign for the last time and slowly drifted out to sea. The marks on the sign were as brash as the sign itself. It read, *No retorno,* which means, "No return!" Maybe Captain William Kidd was trying to tell us something!

*****

Being the last man aboard, it was my job to hoist the ladder and tie it off. I began to pull at it but the ladder wouldn't give. There was some sort of resistance like it may have snagged on something beneath. I flopped over the side to shake it loose.

I froze, unable to. I didn't even try. The ladder's lower edge trailed in the churning ocean, and there, I saw it… the hand. The pale blue hand of the evil that haunted me had wrapped itself tightly around the last rung, bouncing on the white caps as it followed the ship. It rode the waves clenched in fury to cast its terror upon me. Then suddenly, the moon ducked behind a cloud and rendered the body powerless. I watched as each finger slowly opened, one by one, releasing the rung and it's hold on the ship. I watched it sink into the deep dark ocean… and it was gone.

"No retorno" sounded pretty good to me!

With the fear that came with knowing the cross I had to bear, or that we all must bear, I dusted myself off and moved on. Survival required perseverance, an uncanny strength in unity. The days and *Knights* of Wicked Lester were not over… they'd only just begun!

With Hawkeye safely on board, we recapture our southern coarse towards Costa Rica and on her word would travel with hopes of finding the one called Swan before the others do.

Running up the sheets (or sails), we tried to forge ahead of a squall that began to push in from the east. According to legend, and Hawkeye's promising knowledge, the key to finding Pavo Realle lay somewhere near Old Providence Island, deep in the Caribbean Sea.

She talked a sailor's tale of a landmark pass few have heard of and even less have traveled. Referred to as "Neptune's Nest" by the older gents, it served as a seasonal gateway to the Island of Pavo Realle. A strange phenomenon it was. It began at a fresh water spring in the middle of the ocean. As the story is told, this remarkable occurrence happened but once a year around mid-July during the summer solstice. A large swell of warm water flowed northwest from the equator, bringing with it the rain. When that warm salty brine would meet the cool emerald waters of the spring, much as how lightning is formed, the dramatic change in temperature would give rise to a rip tide just below the water's surface. This was particularly so along the Bangar Reef where the flux created a water line on top. That smooth and milky trail began at the freshwater spring and led all the way to the shoreline of Pavo Realle. But the hourglass always trickled its time.

Our gravest concern was that we had to make it to Neptune's Nest before the inclement weather had set in. If the storm was a rage, it could wash away the rip tide, the trail, and our only hope of safely finding Pavo Realle for another calendar year. The dawn will soon break to cast it's graceful light on the world.

We prayed, "May the trade winds carry us ahead of the storm."

It would have been a favorable time to sleep since hadn't seen shut eye in days, but I wasn't sure that I could—mired in stress and apprehension. I was deathly afraid of what I might awaken to find... if I woke at all! As if to confirm my fears, right then and there, it began to rain. I looked to the skies with hope.

We were running full sail in the face of showers that gave the linens quite a beating. I couldn't help but wonder, *do we run for our saving grace or are we running from the ghost ship of Malum the Medicine Man and his cursed krewe.* The dreadful irony of it all is that they were one and the same.

We rode into the dawn, thick as thieves, with the threat of "Do or Die Time" preying upon our minds. An hour or more passed as the red skies of morning enlightened us of the oncoming day and the rain moved on.

Feeling like I'd been 'rode hard and put up wet', as Grandpa used to say, I moved with caution toward the ship's helm to get a feel for our whereabouts—I hated not knowing. Within an earshot, I gathered we were fifty nautical miles northwest of the Emerald Spring and the breaking waves.

The sea had been quite kind on our travels thus far but the mollusks that hound us had not… they still came.

"Skinner boat on the horizon," called out one of the Krewe. A 'skinner boat' was a southern slang expression for Bounty Hunters, no doubt looking to cash in on one Barnacle Bill Bedlam. They must have caught our trail in Te Amare. Another fly in the ointment. Their ship was windswept and was gaining ground, but at a closer look was considerably smaller than *Calypso's Revenge.* Surely, they weren't daring or foolish enough to make a stand… but the smell of money always had a funny way of swaying one's good intentions.

I took my eyes and mind off of the oncoming Ship for just a moment to detect a pair of Orca flanking us, giving us a nod. Bloodthirsty creatures they were, not to be trusted. One had a sea lion clenched in its mouth for devour, the other was without. They played peek-a-boo, displaying some choice moves before they bottomed out to feast on their catch.

The Barnacle ordered two sails down to scrub off speed and I wondered, with a ship like *Calypso's Revenge,* we could out run her in a pinch… so why the strange order? I looked to the Barnacle for remedy and all I received was his crooked smile, the one we all knew so well. The one that he always seemed to be wearing when something bad was about to happen.

With reasonable suspicion, Hawkeye cut an eye toward the captain. With a voice drenched in sarcasm, Hawkeye slyly called out, "Barnacle," as if she knew what was coming next… but nothing could've prepared us.

The captain, steadily looming through his telescope, made his decision. "Mr. Newcastle," he called out to his quartermaster, James Newcastle. "Get the grappling gun!"

No sooner had James taken the order than Hawkeye began to whine. "We have a destination to follow and not much time. Why must you toy with them?" She spoke like a parent scolding her young. "Let it go," she said.

"Would love to Hawk. I have no quarrels with these men but they won't 'let it go', you see," exclaimed Barnacle Bill. "Two words: *Bounty Hunter*. They have no intention of leaving empty-handed so we must humor them now or they will follow us all the way to Pavo Realle, he added.

"Humor not humiliate," said Hawkeye. "You can obviously out-run and out-gun them!"

"Yet they still come," Barnacle replied. "Like I said, 'Bounty Hunters'. Whatever scuttle they have to sell will have to be resolved now before we reach Neptune's Nest!" It was his final word. The armory was preparing itself with gunner's taking to positions on instinct not order.

All I kept thinking was that their captain must have had some set of brass monkeys to move on a ship like *Calypso's Revenge*… so we waited.

The ship came along broadside and held position with ours, the Krewe sharpened their cutlery and looked ready to tangle. Without awaiting their intentions, Barnacle made the first move with style… kind of. He climbed from the captains deck down, onto the ship's railing while holding a sail line with one hand. As he gracefully swayed back and forth, wearing that well known grin, he shouted "Love your dingy!" The entire crew roared in laughter. After the dust settled, Barnacle once again threw them a line. Sneering, he said, "Before I condemn a man, I'll walk a mile in his shoes… so when I *do* condemn him, I'm a mile away *and* I have his shoes!"

Right then, on the punch line, as if it were

rehearsed, there occurred a most intimidating sight: every bay door opened on time. The long necks of fifteen black cannons rolled out in unison to stare at them in the face. Everything got deathly quiet—even the birds dared not make a sound.

Mr Bones

BARNACLE

SCARLETT

Boo

Morgan

Chapter 10

Ballad of Ratline Willie

"THIS IS WHERE THE PLOT THICKENS gentlemen," Barnacle Bill Bedlam called out. "Now, what business ye serve with me?" the Barnacle captain said. "You bloody well know why I'm here so we can dispense with the 'how do ya do's"!"

Bill Bedlam's "jeerful" expression dropped to one of disgust as another thorn from a past long forgotten came calling. Into the limelight, he appeared with a stagger, though I was unsure whether his leg was dead or whether he was just dead-drunk.

Ratline Willie Shanks was his name.

A real bottom feeder, the lowest form of plankton, he was. In the mind's eye of the Krewe, he was somewhere between a sea slug and the bile that forms around your mouth when you're parched.

His claim to fame was when he suddenly chopped up his own brother and used him for chum, just to get his boots. A real family man.

Ratline hobbled forward, chewing on a blood orange. Crimson stained his shirt as the juice ran down his scraggly beard that gave off a bit of a cannibal look. In the other hand, he held a warrant bearing the name: Barnacle Bill.

"Well if it isn't Slackjaw Willie the Rat… goin' fishin'?" shouts the Barnacle, followed by more laughter from the Krewe.

"Now tell me, as you stare down the barrels of fifteen of my best long nines, I've got ya *Dead Bang,* just what do you intend to do with that little slip of paper, Ratboy? And remember to speak very carefully!" Barnacle Bill spoke calmly but his voice sounded otherwise.

"My intentions are real!" called out Ratline Willie. "I've been commissioned to find you! It seems there are some people in London that fancy your return… no matter what your conditions lie!" Shanks was prowling for trouble. "They offer riches, silver and gold, plus letters of pardon for your confessors!" In a darker voice he issued his threat, "And that gold is to be mine!"

"I pity the sorry lot of you!" said Barnacle. "The damned, the beggars, and thieves that live their life half as worthlessly as you! You think I can't hear you but I know who you are!" Bill said in a voice that sounded like snake peel. "Best you and your krewe of miscreants move on along while you're still moving at all! By the way… how's your Brother?"

That last line seemed to touch a nerve. It didn't sit too well with Willie as his expression went from ugly to uglier, if that was possible. Feeling a bit scorned, he shouted to his krewe, "Fetch the boy!" The ship's mood turned somber by a gambler's hand as Ratline Willie played the ace card he'd been holding.

Four men came from below deck dragging another in shackles. A smaller gent, maybe even a boy. I couldn't tell for sure because he was hooded. They paraded him around at gunpoint for show just to prove his worth.

Ratline Willie Shanks ripped the hood from the kid's head like a magician unveiling his latest trick. A painful trick it was, it was one of our own, a *Brethren,* a boy named Seahunter.

The lad was the only son of the pirate, Lord Turtle Brit Belvoir. He was in service aboard the *Leucosia* for Bloody Bob Carver, last I heard. Turtle Brit came running to the railing at Barnacle's side, completely unaware of his son's capture. His eyes turned cold, like a dead man, when he witnessed that the victim was his boy. You could hear the hum of retribution amongst the Krewe, as Seahunter was known as a favorite son. That time, I was afraid Ratline Willie had played his last card.

The Barnacle offered his console with a hand on Brits shoulder, he re-enforces his support to the pirate. "Fear not Lord Brit. I'll let no harm come to your boy! Shanks is as witless as he is coward… time to light the fires!" In a pause, Barnacle murmured to his Turtle friend, "Do you think he remembers the *Singapore Sling?"*

To explain: young Seahunter fancied the art

of prestidigitation, sleight of hand. The *Singapore Sling* is a trick taught to him by his pirate father—how to shiftily escape from shackles (in case he would ever have a need for such information). On that note, without flinch, Barnacle Bill Bedlam made the first move.

"Avast ye Ratline, be ye pirate or turncoat, saint or sinner? The choice be yours!"

"You know me Bedlam," said Willie with an acrid tone. "I pirate these waters from here to Costa Rica, nearly twenty years now… we've met!"

"Well then you must know that you've broken the Pirates' Code," Bill Bedlam replied gruffly. "Article Five, *Taking Up Arms,* that boy is *Brethren…* and you know it," he said.

Just then, in a rather eerie moment, Ratline Willie let go a shriek of rebuttal with the soulless voice of a specter, *"I Don't Bide Under Your Flag, I Don't Live By Your Code!"*

"Then you shall die by it!" shouted Captain Barnacle.

He leaned in towards Turtle and Krewe, muttering under his breath. Unable to discern every word, yet still hearing all I needed to hear, I discerned his message: "Quartermaster Newcastle has armed the grappling gun. We'll get a hook on the boy then Ratline Willies' gonna stop breathing!" It was the final word spoken by Barnacle Bill Bedlam, in a monotone voice that was laced with aggravation.

The four men cocked the hammers of their pistols, all of which were pointed at the head of young Seahunter, to entice us. The Barnacle called out, "Alright Shanks… I'll be your gambit! Here's how I see it, you and I at a duel of swords. When I win, the boy goes free fair and square. On the improbability that you win, I shall lay down my sword and go peacefully no questions ask. What say you Willie Boy?"

Willie paused in thought, masking a look of worry with a cold stare while he nervously fondled the handle of his sword. His thoughts were short, his decision evident as he pulled out the sword he'd been fingering.

"The rapture is near Bedlam! Like a poppet, you will dance to your death… this I promise! And you know what be causing it?" Willie asked, his voice grated sarcastically as his crewmen threw a gangplank in between ships. "Because I *never liked you anyway,*" he belted. Without pause, the battle ensued.

Sparks ignited in broad daylight as the tinny sound of steel on steel echoed over the water. The Barnacle didn't have much trouble guiding the dance because of Willie's gimp, but Ratline kept swinging on. All eyes were focused on the two fighting pirates as the heckles grew louder. Even the four gunmen turned to stare, and that's when 'Plan B' took effect.

It must be said that the one significant thing that fascinated me the most about pirates was their shear passion for cheating death. The most remarkable antics of chivalry… or stupidity… that my eyes had ever seen have occurred in the company of pirates. Well let's just say, I'd seen a lifetime of it.

Sleight of hand. All the right pawns were immersed in the trickery of one hand while the other beheld a different ploy. With a pirate's panache, the gallant escape of young Seahunter was nothing short of wonder as I watched with bright eyes. It seemed no matter what age I grew into or how my cards in life scattered, these daring escapades always kept me young.

As their men were diverted, Seahunter backed two paces with a slithery step. Barnacle called out, "Now Turtle!" In the midst of all the confusion, Turtle Brit shouted to his son, "Singapore Sling!" and that's when I saw it!

A strange shadow appeared in the crystal blue waters beneath us. It moved away quickly, just enough to show itself, just enough to make me want to turn my head a little too late.

I looked back to see the shackled hands of our Brother Seahunter held high in the air, like he's reaching for the sun. Just then, the sound of the grappling gun went off in my ear. Shots started firing. The grappling hook wrapped their stunsail and swung back like a whip to snag young Seahunter as he hurriedly jumped in it's path. It was just enough to thrust him back aboard our ship, landing on his behind as the malay continued.

Ratline took an eye and saw that the boy had been lifted. His temper began to storm.

As Willie looked away, Barnacle seized the

moment. With his sword he whacked the back of the Rat's good leg like a kid playing with a switch he had broken from a nearby tree.

The sting came with a cringe, in turn causing Shanks to lose his footing to fall backwards into the water below. With the two ships still in sway, the water rat drifted from the gangplank a good few yards. He would have to swim for it. But the opportunity never came as the conflict took a grisly turn.

Shanks was struggling to tread water, trying to make his way back to the ship when the ghostlike black shadow from my recollect returned to call.

I could see it clearer as it rose—it was the Orca from the depths. But I only saw the one, I knew not where the other had gone. She must have wet her appetite with the sea lion and was now on the hunt for an entrée. Indeed, it was a bad time to be swimming... a bad time to be Ratline Willie!

His krewe scrambled for their spears to keep the killer whale from their captain. Willie kept paddling, he didn't know what hunted him in the water where he swam. His men seemed to hold the Orca's attention, at least for a little while, with their pokes and jabs, which gave Ratline a few seconds more.

Then again, in life it came—the Hammer of God, another callous reminder from Mother Nature of just how insignificant we humans are in this world. I could hear their men crow with foolish conviction, believing that they'd outsmarted the beast... but one never profits from assumption.

Soon came the pang of regret and looking back, it left me paralyzed.

The focus of attention had shifted. All men paused in their efforts. The scene became as silent as a church. I saw Barnacle Bill on the gangplank take to one knee with his hand outstretched toward Ratline cursing him to swim faster. At first, I didn't know why.

The water began to wake about fifty yards out off the port side, this I saw. What started as a ripple became a swell, moving water to whitecaps. The Barnacle's shouts were loud and mighty to hastily goad Willie on, but the Rat could swim no faster.

That which was mocked became the obvious when chilled to the bone, as the monstrous black dorsal crested the water directly toward us, directly at Ratline Willie.

There was only seconds then. Shanks splashed on just a few feet more from the Barnacles hand. The men were close enough to see the panic in Willie's eyes.

Thirty feet long and eight tons came quickly—the black bull of death. No one dared breathe... they could help him no more.

The next few seconds would never be erased from my memory.

I could hear Willie pant and gasp, taking on water, fighting himself. Then like a ghost, the fin of the great whale disappeared below the surface into the deep—out of sight.

Ratline was within Barnacle's grasp when the first hit came. With his last breath he reached for the hand of Barnacle Bill and was knocked off coarse with a bump. He stood up in the water, his eyes glazed over as his nose began to bleed. The man was still alive but the whale had taken his good leg and blood stained the sea.

He dove for Barnacle's hand one last time before he let go of his life. I wished I had never fallen victim to watch, wished I had never looked him in the eye when death dragged him under.

The shrill curdling scream was heard momentarily before it was cut to silence as the massive jaws snapped the man at the waist in a fit of rage and revolt. Immediately, the beast dragged him down into the dark abyss. I just stood and shook, hemmed in a state of shock while feeling its presence beneath my feet.

To prove their strength and cunning, the first

Orca (the decoy) returned to the surface to mark its territory. She swam a bold path alongside of the bounty hunter's ship and the men that provoked her. On her back, baking in the sunlight was the severed half corpse of Ratline Willie, displayed for all to see. With a flick of her tail she took it under and was gone.

Out-fooled the fool, the wicked the wiser—as one whale ran decoy the other engaged the attack. That's the last anyone ever saw of Ratline Willie Shanks.

No words were spoken between ships. Every man present stood locked in a surreal daze over the ghastly show. At any given moment the Barnacle could've sunk 'em! With a word and the spark of a fuse, he could've put them all to death… but he didn't. He just stood there like the rest of us. A leering eye, frozen in time, he stood with his men as we watched the current carry away the other ship in silence, drifting on out of sight… in peace.

Legend has it, the hunter became the hunted—a fearful reminder to mankind to never underestimate the intelligence of God's creatures. For they may be smarter than you think!

Chapter 11

How Come it Never Rains

AS FATE WOULD ALLOW, THIS HORRID encounter had left us only thirty knots off our mark and thirty miles from the crystal blue pools of Neptune's Nest en route to Pavo Realle.

I rested myself for a spell on the ships railing. With arms crossed and head down I gazed at the brilliant colors of the coral reefs that passed below my eyes as I desperately tied to clear my thoughts. The colors seem to bleed into one as we suddenly caught a good pull off of a tailwind, pitching us faster. There was still plenty of day to squander.

Before too long the spring was in view. It was just as I pictured it in my head, ice blue water rising from below. You could see it bubbling, overflowing into a perfect circle nearly one hundred yards wide. Just beyond it the river of salvation awaited. The trail, the rip tide that would lead us to the island was apparent. It was just as Hawkeye described.

She was standing at the ship's aft, shouting orders, "Thirty degrees to the port side!" she yelled and we fell in line with the sun and sea, in perfect tune with the tide.

We were well on our way then.

Within an hour, we arrived at a patch of clouds, defending it's circle to strangely shelter this very spot of ocean. Within it's foggy cloak laid the Island of Pavo Realle. Finally arrived! Wrapped in it's thick milky haze, we anchored down and headed for the longboat.

Hawkeye got us there, that's for sure, but finding Cygnus on the Island... we soon found out that we were on our own. How would you find someone that doesn't wanna be found? Why, through the looking glass, of course.

I stood there, free at hand as the Krewe continue to secure the ship and prep the longboat. Finding me in a somber state, my ol' friend Shotglass Sam chimed in on cue as he has always did whenever my mind was cloudy.

"Hellaye," said he. With my back to him, I continue to lean on the rail, waiting to vent and in need of a friend.

"I'm afraid I don't have any peanuts for you my friend... down on my luck, as it were," I said to him. "Another fine mess eh?" I whined childishly. And then I gave in, unloading all of my woes on this poor bird's ear. I babbled on about dark voyage, the things I'd done and seen. I told him that I bore the curse of the Skeleton Krewe. I even told him of the Tommyknocker, the specter that had been haunting my every move.

"It's a bitter pill. I'm marked for death for a

swindle that occurred long before I was born!" I said to Sam, resigned to my fate. "But he knows me now, the Wicked Lester knows my name! I was nearly drowned by his evil," I said and sighed. "Who's ever gonna believe me? Been towed under water and strangled by the grisly remains of a pirate that's been dead nearly a hundred years or more!" I tried to joke, speaking with a fool's nervous chortle. "Darn nearly lost my life, no one even knows."

The response came in two words that put me in a dead cold shiver, "Sin piedad." But the voice that was heard was not that of the bird. I turned to find her standing there, haloed by the sun. It was the ever lovely Scarlett DeVille with Sam selfishly nestled on her shoulder. She had been there the whole time, she heard every note. For a brief moment I become boyishly lost in the tranquility of her stare. Her eye's were crystal aquamarine, I remember—even more vivid than the sea and sky that surrounded her. She began to speak an offering of confidence. With few words she simply put it to rest.

"He knows young Mr. Tyler," said Lady Scarlett. "The *Haints* have been after Barnacle for nearly twenty years now. I've seen his nightmare—I've felt his pain. For many moons I've overheard him while in solitude, the quiet conversations with Malum and his disciples. As the years passed, their terror seemed to cultivate and grow just as their stronghold gripped upon all who bore the curse of Carbonados!" She sighed and cocked her head to one side, eyeing me as she spoke. "One in particular, he calls by name—Slippery Pete is the name I hear most," Scarlett said.

There was a moment or two of dead silence then she quietly wished me well as I turn to board the longboat. "Courage is all you're left with now," I heard her say. As I straddled the ladder and began to climb, I could still hear Scarlett's call to me. "Never show your weakness, never let them know you're afraid," said she.

Standing on the longboat looking up into the sun, I could barely see her wave us on. With half a grin and my sad attempt at southern charm, I left her with a question as we pushed off for Pavo Realle… because I plainly wanted to know.

I said, "Why does it never rain, it only pours?"

My words brought tears to her eyes but she still managed a smile. We muddled on through the haze with each man staring at the other while sharing the same disquieted look, the look of the cursed.

It was without saying that soon, the cloud cover would break to reveal an Island we knew very little of. Clearly, we would need to keep to mind, keep our focus.

The Isle rose up in a hurry, filling my senses with the smell of begonia as they beautified the coastline of this strange place. We washed ashore with not the slightest notion of where to begin our search.

No sooner than our Krewe of fifteen men set foot to sand than we came upon a trail of footprints. We followed them on instinct like the blind leading the blind and must've tracked the lone steps nearly a mile before we stumbled upon an object buried in the sand. It was an old wooden toy, weathered and worn—bilbo catcher they're called. The old cup and ball with a string attached for honing hand to eye coordination must've washed up with the tide.

"Let me see that," spouted a disgruntled Bill Bedlam. He intently stared at the object, caressing it tightly in hand as if it were his own. I would later come to find that it had been—strange but true. "This was once mine... when I was a boy," Barnacle quietly confessed as he continued his boyhood look of fond remembrance. One would have never believed it, had it not held the letters *BB* crudely carved into the handle of the toy. But then again, the way the trip had unfurled, there was nothing that surprised me anymore at that point.

Barnacle pocketed the item without question and we resumed our task of following the trail of footmarks. The paces led from sand to jungle as the hunt continued for the long lost friend. The tangle was rich in venomous snakes that hung from the trees. Poisonous spiders spun webs along our path. The sanctuary of the tropics was well preserved there and in the order of a dominating breed.

As the trail led us deeper into woods, the steps became less visible though the path remained the same. Through brush and mire, we arrived at a parting of trees. Suddenly, every sod among us sighed at the panoramic beauty of what was hidden in the trees. It was a picturesque setting, like a piece of art that had been painted on canvas, too real to the touch. A secluded lagoon with sapphire blue waters danced in the sunlight. Sea salt-colored sand sequined a serene pool. Swaying palm trees bowed down over graceful blue as if to listen to whispers from the sea. To complete this painting, the remains of an old Spanish Galleon had found its final resting place where she peacefully slept with her nose down in a sandbar. Through weather and time, only sections of her were left standing. The relics of the ship's stern served as an arched entrance to the lagoon. The ship's name still proudly hung intact, suspended above our heads like a boardwalk sign. It read, "Adventure Galley." Strange, but I felt as if I'd heard the name before.

We passed 'neath the sign with a sense that

we'd entered a carnival—through the hull of the stern where the rudder once was to patiently spill out into a scenic daydream that was filled with beauty and wonder. Every inch was covered in color and life.

For a brief period the Krewe seem to lose sight of why we were there—so caught up in the moment, a feeling of frivolousness overtook them to run wildly and playfully settle into that little slice of paradise.

Still shadowed in suspicion, the captains, Bloody Bob, Morgan the Hook, and Barnacle disallowed their taste of tranquility to continue in lieu of a cautious investigation of the surroundings. It wasn't long before another piece of the puzzle presented itself, and this clue came with a song.

While crawling through the belly of this magnificent relic where most treasures still lay intact, as did the souls that left them behind and with no means of disrespect, we pilfered a few trinkets along the way. After all, we were pirates. I managed to pocket a few doubloons and what looked to be a shiny gold locket.

In the center of a table sat a fancy brass balance, teetering in kilter from the booty it held. On one side, a swatch of sheet music had been covered in gold, old and worn and barely legible. *Amazing Grace,* I think it was.

The finder had his mind on the gold, so after a swift glance about him, he threw the swatch away. The song was in full swing when the hand of Bloody Bob Carver caught him by the wrist.

Bloody Bob snatched the cloth sheltering it from sight and, cowering away like a poor man hiding his pence, it became obvious that the omen was meant for him.

He stood with his back towards us as he made us aware of the gift from his mother. "It was her favorite hymn," he said, arm raised to swear in truth. "I used to play it for her on an old dulcimer when I was eleven years old." His voice had dropped to a whisper. I began to wonder, was this a strange coincidence or was it a mind game birthed from the macabre. Seconds later, I got my answer.

I had wandered off from the others to explore the ship's remains when the Tommyknockers arrived. I fished in my pockets to inspect what was mine. Curiously, I open the locket and I barely saw the image of a young lady when I noticed that it was inscribed. But it was too dark where I stood to make out the inscription. I moved closer to the light coming from the porthole and held the object inches from my eye, like a blind man trying to read. Suddenly, my fingers turned to ice as my body froze—I read the inscription. It said, *Sin piedad.*

Just as the words took meaning, the picture, the lovely young lady of the locket, melted into the image of the nightmarish specter that had cursed me. I dropped the locket, exposing the skull of a dead pirate just as it's lower jaw began to chatter. Blood froze in my veins—I knew I was being watched.

Without even looking, I could see faces through the portholes and could feel their eyes upon me.

Inches away, the faces of the dead filled the round windows, desperately leering at me through the looking glass. I didn't dare look and trembled as I kept my eyes focused downward upon my feet. My hope was that they would go away and I waited for a chance to run for the light of day and a white sandy beach.

I raised my heavy head just enough to see the only object within the room – an old pew like from a church, dark and rusty, covered in the sands of time. Upon it lay a single dead snapdragon, ghostly white – it watched me.

I began to hear something within the room. It was music that sounded like a stringed instrument – a dulcimer that played *Amazing Grace.* I was once again consumed in fear but only for a short while. Thankfully, my moment of dread was broken by the pirate king, Barnacle Bill Bedlam.

Strangely, he stood there without course, action, or word. Suddenly the music stopped and the faces vanished. His response then came, systematic and sure. He looked right through me, cut his eyes to the porthole, and then to the bench where the dead flower sat. He knew… he finally knew.

Barnacle took the snapdragon from the pew and crushed it beneath his boot, looked right at me, and then just walked away. I followed without a blink to make for the white sandy beach to warm the chills from my spine… but they just grew colder.

Chapter 12

Twilight's Last Gleam

WE SEARCHED FOR THE NEAREST opportunity for escape from this magnificent ruin. The moment we did, he was waiting. Seven foot tall, dark skinned, and bedecked with a finger bone necklace. Two human skulls dangled as knockers from his sash. War paint covered his face like a tribal skull. He looked just like the reaper of death. It was "The Medicine Man," Wicked Lester Banks himself.

Was it flesh or fantasy? No one really knew if he was still part of the living. His fingers were abnormally long with nails that looked like daggers as he used them to point out each of us. He stood there, silent, staring cold as a dead man, making it hard to tell whether he was real or a trick of the mind.

Within a click, he looked Barnacle in the eye then cast us spellbound with his evil smile. The air grew too thick to breathe. Like black magic he blinked his eyes and thousands of tiny scorpions surround us—mounds of them, squirming to encircle our feet.

He laughed in our face as the lethal black bugs began to crawl upon us, slowly moving onto our skin. Captive by the heart of voodoo itself, we were unable to move. Too frail to fend off one scorpion, much less the lot of them.

His voice growled a deep resonance as he posed his threat on the cursed few. "No tener piedad, No mostrarse misericordioso! You've pilfered Carbonados treasures, slighted the family name, and all it's worthy!" he rumbled fiercely as his leer slowly panned from one man to the next. "You're Jack Rackham's rats aren't you?"

By now the deadly black insects had reached knee level and shock had set in. We trembled and shook, awaiting the sting of a thousand scorpions. Suddenly, I felt as if I was a few steps closer to becoming a dead man as it became clear to me—there would be no way out of this. I felt the creatures 'neath my clothing as they gradually neared places best left alone. The whole of it made my shakes worsen.

Lester looked to the sky with his hands in the air like he was praying to his God. He then let go in a rant of anger, "A life sacrifice for another, man's treachery and greed. Curse your Skeleton Krewe! The profits you thieved were mine," said he. 'You have no inkling about the demons you've unleashed… in me!"

Suddenly, he began to mumble in gibberish to chant in a language I did not know -- a tribal tongue perhaps, from who knows where. His cold dark eyes played no diversion to what came next—his mercenaries.

As if the bloody scorpions weren't enough! I snapped at myself. *I'm at death's door knockin'—it seems my life has exceeded the limits God granted. He holds us all tightly in his fists of bone.*

Then his very image began to replicate. One by one, dark skeletal figures came into view, nodding in from the bushes all around us. Los Muertos it was. Out numbered by the apparitions and buried in scorpions, we held as the dead began to close in. Our final moments were upon us when our captain did something I never would have expected, and for that I will always regard and honor him. Be it short fused or chivalrous, in our state of frenzy, Barnacle Bill Bedlam finally broke and called him out. He stared into the eyes of his krewe. He could see the anguish—tired of shaking, tired of the nightmare and the torment, I couldn't sweat one more bullet.

To spare us all the worst and the bitter anticipation of a certain death, Barnacle pulled the punch that he knew would set off Wicked Lester. He'd had enough. I guessed he'd figured the only way to lift the curse was to pay it. Scorpions flew from his sleeves, as with a quick draw, he pulled the pistol he wore on his chest and aimed it dead square at the head of the medicine man. "Come time to die," growled Bill Bedlam to the man of voodoo.

By that time I was shaking uncontrollably,

terrified, eyes wide, and my lips chanting a nursery rhyme that my Grandpa used to recite to me when I was very young and couldn't sleep for fear of the dark.

"I will walk upon the sea, let the summer shine on me, lead me shelter from the storm and the courage to keep me warm."

I repeated the words over and over again, hoping, like Grandpa's promise, that it would make this nightmare go away!

In a flash of black powder, though for me everything seemed to move in slow motion, the trigger was pulled and the boom from the Barnacle's favorite pistol cracked the sky. I could see the lead ball leave the barrel in a blaze of fire and smoke. The bullet pierced the forehead of Wicked Lester Banks to send him backward, but not off his feet. The loud bang did us in—it sparked the sting of a thousand scorpions.

The pain wrenched my body like a bolt of lightning from Neptune's hand, igniting every nerve with a searing pain worse than death itself. I dropped to my knees in spasms, waiting for my life's fire light to extinguish. Laying there with my vision fading, at the last sight I saw that Malum was not dead—no wound, no blood. The bullet passed him through like a ghost. My last remembrance in that gleam of twilight was his twisted laugh that echoed in the darkness of my mind as I slowly slipped away.

At once, there came a light, burning through the lids of my eyes that were crusty and closed.

But it wasn't a heavenly light, no hand of God awaited me thus far. Still, as I laid in the afterglow, I reveled in its warmth and comfort—as a mothers touch, or so I would assume.

It was… it was the sun—the dawn of a brand new day. I was alive.

The Krewe awoke to find a beautiful sunrise that crested the horizon with amber starbursts that lit a blue Caribbean tide. We all stood and gazed as if it were the first time. No evil demigod, no ravenous spirit of the dead that waited to feed on us and interestingly, not a scorpion in sight. Gone without a trace, without a scratch or sting, they had all completely vanished, leaving the Krewe bewildered but still alive. For that, I was grateful to find I had been wrong. It truly was a heavenly light from the hand of God we witnessed on that day. I took the time to embrace it.

With fate pending and the murmurs of the scare hanging on everyone's lips, Barnacle decided it was time to move on, rather than tug at that thread despite the fact we knew that we were not free men. The Curse of Carbonados still marked our names.

We second guessed our way down a less traveled path in hopes to keep our noses clean, but it didn't last long. The island had eyes that moved with us, or so it seemed. We had only stepped forty yards out from the wreckage of the *Adventure Galley,* barely to crest the next strand of beaches, when the wind carried an unfamiliar voice. Another turn in this maze of mysteries on the Island of Pavo Realle.

"Having fun with the natives are we?" it said. The searing words sent a spike right through me!

He was a crooked man that walked a crooked path who appeared out of nowhere. The man rested within our periphery just... fishing. The distant stranger sat in his boat with his back towards us, casting and reeling as if we were not there at all. But the boat was not on the bay, it queerly rested ten feet from the tide buried in the sand. Still he huddled aboard her foolishly fighting his rod and reel with nothing to show but an empty hook. He was in an ocean of the unconventional, a pillar of unconformity. He loved his boat but not the water. He dreamed in color but lived a life within a black and white world, secluded and alone.

I don't know how, but in the twinkling of an eye I knew who it was just by the weight of his words, poignant and powerful. It was in fact the misfit sage we had been in search of all along—the Swan, Cygnus. The long lost friend and the key to this voyage of salvation. It seemed the the poor sod that we had sailed the sea to find… had instead found us.

He fumbled about the boat without a look toward us until all men were within earshot—a move that would ensure his time would not be wasted. Then he spun with a shrewd swagger, cutting both eyes on Barnacle and Bloody Bob Carver. They shared a timely pause for the years and a warm smile of remembrance.

Those men divvied the commemoration, a brief cycle of 'remember when's' then they rounded the horde, and prepared to leave. With the feel of the devil's due on approach, time was a frill not in our favor.

We trailed our guide through woods and wetlands as we looked for sanctuary—a place to rest our heads. The hike went on for a good hour yet the trail was always within eyeshot of the beach. Oddly I felt as if we were going in circles. Deep within the isle's tropical veneer, buried in palm and thicket, was the hideaway of the ambiguous Swan. Feeling a bit out of place, the surroundings looked strangely familiar. A curious dwelling seemingly built for a gnome, small, tight to the fit. It bared the appearance of an old rum shack or smuggler's hold. The inside was jumbled with trinkets and clutter, mementos from his life and others.

He had saved everything.

Secretly, he lit some candles as a call to meeting… it's bullet to bone time, the game of truths had begun. The rum was poured and passed around as the mumble and chatter began to subside. We sat there with cold hands and warm hopes for the answer to a curse, an answer we may never find. With knowing eyes, Cygnus showed a side of compassion but his prudence would be to our misfortune. He knew… he knew everything—the lines that were crossed, the bridges burned, even the stars we would have to ignite just to save our own lives.

Whiskey boiled in a pot over a small flame. He kept a close watch as he stirred and tasted and tweaked to perfection the concoction he'd created. All the while, he yammered on, spinning his yarns. A gruesome tale of irony it was. It went something like this.

"I can smell the muddy waters of home running like a river in your mind. Once again, they carry the ghosts of your adolescence," said Cygnus. "Do you remember as children how we used to run down by that livery near the Fisher's Wharf? There would always be that transient there, old blind man Fulton sitting idly by feeding the birds he thought were there but never were. Remember how he loved to frighten us -- how he loved to rattle our impressionable little minds with the tale of the killing of the horses?"

Chapter 13

Man of Many Talons

"THROUGH SIGHT THAT COMES SOLELY from sound, the old man knew when the stable hand would put down an animal that was tired or lame. It took place always at the shank of the day when the sun started to fade. He heard the horrific sounds of the struggle, the kicking, the screaming of the horses as they faced pain of death… remember?" Cygnus stared at us from the corner of his eye and continued. "Some years past, by strange coincidence, there came a day when I found my feet back down on the Fisher's Wharf." Cygnus paused for a moment.

"My memory came in waves as I reluctantly stopped to stare at the abandoned old edifice that was once the livery stable. I heard the sound of the foghorn whistle to signify the end of a working day in the harbor and the coming of night. I could see the lighthouse fire from the neighboring isle. I remembered feeling the cool chill of dusk settle in around me when the spirits came.

"Just as the old blind man had said, 'from within

the walls I heard screaming… the screaming of the horses'. My feet turned to clay, I was grounded I couldn't move. The longer I stood there the louder the sound grew. It seemed so real, so close, so evil." Cygnus sighed. "Finally my infantile instincts took hold and I turned tail to run. I only made it as far as the paddock when I caught a strange sight. Two feet sticking out from behind a carriage in the alley, shaking wildly like a fish out of water. I didn't want to know, yet I reluctantly moved closer and closer just the same," he said sadly. "It became clear to me just what ailed the owner of the legs – it was not a drunken stupor, no. He was dying. As I rounded the corner I saw the old man inside of me. White hair worn and weary, many lines on my face. Lying there in a puddle of mud I saw… myself twenty or more years down the road. The screaming I had heard from the livery was not horses at all… it was me."

I watched as a shudder passed down Cygnus' spine.

"I stared into my own eyes and felt the same torture and pain. I watched myself battling death's demons for my last gasp, screaming franticly at someone or something as if we were being chased. With a look of gloom and arm outstretched, I reached for the hand of my elder to help...a tic too late. He had flat lined, stiff as a board. A life lost. I saw my own humanity bleed out of me withered in shame, in agony and alone wallowing in that dank alley."

"From all around I could hear the onlookers

start to flock. They gawked, sputtered and scoffed at the tattered remains of a wasted life… my life, which explained a very distraught Cygnus. Through the wake of callous catcalls, my ears bent on a single voice, a voice your ear does rue, Bill Bedlam," said Cygnus. "It said, 'Sin piedad'... no mercy. Soon, all of the stranger's voices began to pick up on it, chanting it louder and louder. You see, truth be not kind, Barnacle. I stole from Carbonados too! Another time, another place but my blood runs as black as yours!"

The jaded confessions of Cygnus made me shudder. The fire of hope had burned out, our dreams had moved on. It seemed the man of many answers that we'd braved the seas to find was no better off—just another poppet filled with needles and pins.

So, as we stood there in the shadows of doubt, the men of *Calypso's Revenge* began to stir in their own resentment as the scene unfolded. I knew of Bill Bedlam's ill temper… it wouldn't be long before the bottom dropped out.

I watched his face change from Sodom to Gomorrah as his patience wore thin and that wild eyed gazed look returned to his stare. Then suddenly, he spoke.

"They say lack of hope will make a man brave." Barnacle Bill raised his eyebrows as he slowly pulled his rather large German flintlock from its holster and quietly placed it on the table, barrel pointed straight at Swan's Heart. He then rested his right hand on the gun while his fingers nervously tapped on the barrel. His eyes never left Cygnus. It was a test of will's.

With a twitch, Cygnus stammered, "Do you believe in dreams?" No one dared speak—the silence was deafening as we waited out the pause. Finally, Cygnus continued. "There's a place where the real and surreal collide. A place where the thin balance of two worlds are survived only by the powers of one's boundless imagination, courage and valor. A place... only in a dream. There, an angel awaits—one with the power to set our souls free."

"The Sea Spirit?" Barnacle Bill Bedlam eyed him.

"Aye," said Cygnus, "MerAme she's called, The Spirit of the Sea."

The round table of benedictions had peaked then was soused with a whisper and a prayer. So there it was, our new purpose, our new destination. We had no choosing nor say, our lives hang in the balance. So we prepare to embark on that blue frontier for the last time with darkness in our eyes and our souls uncertain. We were just a small flame that would soon run into a red night fire, our curse still remained thicker than blood, and our resolve just as determined.

We emerged from the hobbit home of Swan to see the last hour of daylight and to feel the sting of the hoodwink. Feelings of Deja vu were there for good reason—we were back at square one. Indeed, we had come full circle of the island and Cygnus lived in a section of wreckage from the *Adventure Galley*. He laughed as he called himself "foolishly clever," or so he thought from his manner of cloaking his home while we all mentally plotted his demise for time ill spent. He was taken aboard, nonetheless.

So we set sail to roam into the night and leave behind the island of Pavo Realle in the sunset. From the shadows I watched as Cygnus went from snake oil salesman to human, standing alone while he wept, watching his home slowly fade from sight, knowing in his heart he would never return. Our heading was to Negril, Jamaica. We sailed into the surreal, to an oasis of angels.

"There we'll find MerAme, we'll get the Talisman, we'll get our lives back!" shouted Morgan the Hook.

The Haitian Tribe of the Holy that possessed the Talisman Kuma-wani, the Sea Spirit, inhabited an isle on the coast of Negril. When the Great Hurricane of 1780 consumed the entire Caribbean, a Tsunami sunk their small Isle within minutes. It dove five hundred feet below sea level into the deep blue with the Tribe, their families, and the Kuma-wani. This much the men already knew. But there was more to the story, I soon found out.

"Legend has it that Neptune took pity upon their people. He touched the tribe and all it's inhabitants giving them a new life under the sea with lungs to breathe and fins to fly. They would also live eternally. The Kuma-wani is Holy. He who holds it holds salvation and possesses it's power, it's spirit... the Spirit of the Sea," Morgan continued.

"Question!" spouted Bill Bedlam. "How does

one barter with an Angel? How do I convince her to give up the amulet, the demigod of her people, I wonder?"

Cygnus leaned in with his cold blank stare and growled. "If my mind's eye serves me well, you won't even have to say please!" He turned and walked away.

We soon inherited the wind. I could hear the sweet music as the sails cracked, soaring our ship onward while carving a brazen trail all the way to Jamaica. With the dark night closing in, I felt compelled to grab an hour of slumber, should nerves and apprehensions allow. I was a bit apprehensive—Tommyknockers always thrilled to light in times when we were weak and vulnerable... these things I knew.

Bearing that thought in mind, I moved on. All signs were seemingly on coarse so I ducked down below deck to find a slip to slide into and perhaps sleep a while. A select few who were left to man their posts had made it easy to find a open bunk. My pockets filled with false security as I moved to choose the one nearest the captain's quarters, thinking I'd be invisible and out of harm's way... a foolish notion.

I pulled myself into the top hammock by the breezeway near the captain's door. Hung on the wall across from me, I noticed a rather large mirror set in a fancy gold frame. I thought it odd at first that such a large mirror would hang by the captain's door, but to all who know Bill Bedlam, the question answered itself.

With eyes closed, I fussed and fidgeted to try desperately to nod off, but nothing seemed to work. An uncomfortable silence, not common for that time of night, kept me awake. I quickly decided it would be best to not to question or tug at that thread… for fear of what may come.

As I laid there swinging back and forth in my hammock, I heard the door to the captain's cabin creak open. It took all that I had to peel my eyes for a look. The door was cracked only slightly, nothing but darkness was seen inside. Then came a scratching sound ever so lightly… but I noticed.

In a blink, out walked Shotglass Sam with talons dragging across the wood floor as he headed straight for me. I wiped the sweat from my forehead and lay back down, ready to curse that confounded bird as he once again had fooled the fool! Shortly, I realized that he had come to offer comfort. He knew I was here and had come for a visit. Sam perched atop a chair back next to the mirror to watch over me as I slept, "a man of many Talon's," I said and was grateful.

With a friend standing idly by, I was able to get a bit of rest… at least for a short while. Somewhere in the night I was shaken by the sound of more scratching somewhere near where I slept. I took comfort to know it was only Sam so I didn't bother to open my eyes. Instead, I just slept. The sound continued as I shook in my bunk, murmuring at Sam to be quiet. Strangely, it sounded as if he were scratching on glass. It's amazing at just how quickly an evening can go from a whisper to a scream.

The scratching went on and on 'til finally I snapped. I rolled over, armed and ready to yell at my friend Sam, but found myself powerless, unable to yell at all. I was not awake nor was I asleep—I was somewhere in between. It was as if I had been caught in a daydream—or in this case, a nightmare. I opened my eyes to see fog steadily rise from the hull of the ship. Sam was nowhere to be found. A white Snapdragon lay on the vacant chair once occupied by Sam. It was bitter cold and I could see my own breath. My eyes cut toward the mirror… and there it was, a grisly sight. The faces of a hundred corpses scratching at the mirror from the inside. The large mirror began to move and bend as the specters forced against it, trying to reach for me. There were the Equipo de los Muertos. They pressed dead faces in to stare me down. But the pressure was too much, I could hear the glass begin to crack. I rolled out of that hammock, bolted down the hallway, and hit the stairs a-runnin', like my tail was on fire. I'd thought I'd gotten away, never knowing that the worst was yet to come.

Chapter 14

A Murder of One

I CLEARED THE LAST STEP TO FIND THE night pitch black and raining. I'll never forget it, what my eyes saw—it was the moment I knew for sure—that moment when I knew we were all going to die.

With the night black as coal, I was not sure the hour. A red moon hid in the darkness cloaked by rain clouds. The wind and rain intensified—it was a hard rain too, the kind that stings the skin. Slowly the blood moon rose.

The Krewe panicked while getting pummeled fiercely from the skies. I saw it all turn red… blood red. This squall didn't bring it's salty Atlantic blue rain. No, it was raining blood, crimson red, pounding our ship and Krewe from above like the gates of Purgatory had opened up just for us. The ship's deck was stained scarlet red, our bodies matted with the blood of evil itself. And then the sharks began to surface.

Right then it came, a loud sound that blew in on the north wind, drowning out the bloody rain.

It was the sound of laughter, the sinful mirth of one Wicked Lester Banks, who reveled in our demise. I watched as Captain Barnacle fought tooth and nail to keep his ship in line and on coarse under perdition's fury.

The wind blew circles around us, creating a water spout one hundred feet high—a giant funnel of blood and sea water that formed above our ship to bear down upon us. Clinging tight to the ship's railing, I gripped the wood though it was hard to hold onto. I could hear the laughter whirling around my head to cause vertigo. Judgment day had arrived!

Amidst all of this rage and ruin, I had the gall to look up into the eye of the storm. It's pipe was a chamber filled with bodies—cursed bodies, those of specters and haunts, victims of misfortune spinning round and round, hundreds flung by the maelstrom. I watched the dead violently tossed about like rag dolls into the sky, poppets of a madman. I prayed aloud, "When will it all end?"

The ghostlike fog had risen from below and slowly made it's way along the main deck. It coiled around each man, one by one as if on the hunt, knowing each one by name. I witnessed the strange apparition go from an enigma to an entity to take on a human form. A pale silhouette passed right through us like water through a sieve then vanished down the corridor below out of sight. On board, the ship was in sheer chaos as we spiraled deeper into our bloodstained realm of madness and delusion.

Through the darkness, a bosun's whistle sounded. Morgan the Hook shouted for the attention of Bill Bedlam. "Shoot the moon!"

"Aye," replied Barnacle without hesitation.

I waited breathlessly, knowing that to *'shoot the moon'* would mean all aboard would deploy a diversionary tactic, including the captain and Krewe. The maneuver was used as a forewarning to oncoming ships of prey. It has also been used as an obnoxious and intimidating 'thumbing of the nose' to vessels of the Royal Navy when least expected. On the captain's word, the gunners aim every cannon on board straight up to the heavens. Upon his command, they fire in unison to rock the sea and sky with an unearthly deafening and blinding white light to create a spectacle that allows pirates an easy getaway behind a wall of black powder and smoke. This would allow the ship to vanish without a trace.

"Shoot the Moon!" shouted Barnacle Bill to his gunners.

Every man on board went to aid to pack a swift and blinding force. A monumental maneuver it was, uniform and rehearsed to perfection—larger than life. By Captains' command it went like this:

"At The Ready!" shouted Morgan to Bill Bedlam. All gunners were in position as the Captain gave command.

"With eyes on the prize!" shouted the Barnacle. All cannons rolled back at once with a loud rumble and one good tug. "And one foot in the grave," he added. Like a dance, the stomp of the gunners' boot on the barrelhead and forty cannons touched the sky. "We'll dance the hempin' jig!" said Barnacle.

Fireworks lit up the night when the gunners sparked, awaiting to blow their fuse. "FOR THE LIFE WE BRAVE!" Bill Bedlam screamed as the glow sticks hit the fuse. Indeed, I remembered it well… it truly was the end of days.

I had just enough time to drop to the floor, curled up into a ball before I covered my ears when Barnacle dealt the final blow. The guns went off in a blaze of glory. I could feel the sound and I feared it would be our last. The heavens erupted with a mighty wrath, flashed bright as white lightning as the guns converted the night into daylight.

Shots filled the eye of the storm to rupture it's soulless core. It burst into a fiery mixture of smoke and flame that encircled our ship like a tomb. When bodies burn, the stench is not soon forgotten.

The final moment came with a vengeance as wind and wave grew more turbulent. I could hear the ship's hull crack, yet she kept up the fight with her keel digging into the storm. Rising from the deep blue depths, the scourge breathed—we could feel it beneath us, knocking at the bilge. The ship began to sway and rock, leaning heavily toward the port side.

The heavy load took its toll on Barnacle's sweet *Revenge* with little wonder why! It was "Equipo de los Muertos" that was coming for us! The Krewe of dead pirates rose from the ocean to cling and claw at the ship, one corpse after the other. Sailors grabbed their pistols and muskets and immediately began to fire down into the pack of cadavers, hoping to shake them off, but it didn't take. The main mast was aimed at ten o'clock and turning fast. They were trying to capsize us! I remained still, arms holding tightly to the railing. The ship was almost on her side and plowing, red waters flooding the deck and me along with it! On that night *Calypso's Revenge* went down.

We were helpless against the curse, pulled under with an enormous force as if death's hand had a hold on us. I held on so tightly that my arms were numb. As I fought to hold my breath, I felt the sudden brush from a hammerhead across my back as we dove into the dark abyss. In a shot, we were bottom up and looking down but we never stopped turning!

By the grace of God, I spotted a light—something was in our favor. The weight, balance, and buoyancy of the ship kept her turning on a horizontal axis. Lucky for us, the ship's rum locker was located on the starboard side and when the right side bellied up, the weight of the rum pulled her right back under. The harder we went down the harder we bobbed back to the surface. The ship spit water and smoldered as the sea barrel rolled a two hundred and fifty ton pirate ship.

When the smoke had cleared and had been washed away, it took the nightmare with it—nearly every trace. Captain Barnacle popped up out of the water hat on with hands still at the wheel though he bled from the leg—a rather bad injury. From the naked eye it looked as if he'd been bitten by a shark but it was difficult to tell for certain. Bristling in distress, Scarlett instantly arrived, toting a bottle of rum and some tattered wet gauze. The bite was crescent shaped on the back of his leg that was deep and serrated, surely an animal bite. With a motherly touch, she wrapped the leg tightly to stop the bleeding as he sat there and clenched his teeth, occasionally nipping from the bottle.

The ship rose to blue skies and a warm sun that waited for us upon the horizon. The storm had passed—it was over and everything was gone. No storm, no blood rain, no Wicked Lester. The sea was as calm as the morning tide in spring and we were alive. Indeed, it was by the Grace of God!

The mood broke when a Krewman yelled from below deck, "Barnacle, you'd better come topside." Bill Bedlam laid in the arms of his wife and child—only to insure their safety—and to get patched up at the same time when he heard the call. With sour apprehension, the two captains, Barnacle and Morgan the Hook, rattled and rolled their way down the corridor to the forecastle. I immediately thought of that infamous saying: *When the worst is expected… that's what's begot!*

The three men entered the room to find Cygnus silent and still, without breath or heartbeat. Lester had taken him. That cloudy apparition that had eerily sifted its way through us had finally found what it was looking for. Cygnus' body was sprawled across the dining table, lying atop a bed of dead snapdragons! The deckhand said he found him there kicking and screaming, *"as if he were being chased."*

I could feel the anger brew and witnessed the same in the eyes of Barnacle Bill as he listened to those chilling words. Unexpectedly, he was forced to say goodbye to an old friend. They wrapped his body in a flag taken from the mizzen mast. Not a word was spoken. They chucked him into the blue sea—a proper pirate burial, I presumed.

It's never been easy to lose a friend. It's said that 'time heals all wounds' but the adage is not true. The friendship is merely tucked away, neatly locked in the treasure chest known as a true-friend's heart. It never leaves a person's soul... most just learn to live with it. And so it was with the Barnacle and his friend, Cygnus.

Later, I returned to the forecastle to find Barnacle Bill sitting alone at the table where Cygnus had perished. I eased into one of the chairs, cautious to make not a sound. It was so quiet that I could hear him breathe. Clearly, he was in pain. I didn't say a word simply because I didn't have a word to say. In silence he just sat there, staring at the table covered with dead flowers. Suddenly, I was startled as he abruptly came to life and brushed the flowers from the table with a sweep of his arm. Barnacle glanced behind him, paused, and stared curiously at the tabletop. Something had been etched into the wood—cut by a knife. It said: *Circle of Souls, Bowlegs Bight, MerAme*—Cygnus' final words. Scribed as he died—those words would perhaps save our lives!

Bone-weary, we rolled into the warm sun, heading for Negril—a ship filled with misfits of sage and bound by a will to survive. According to Barnacle, a two-day sail should put us right onto the shores of Jamaica and Moonlight Bay. From there, we would be on our own.

Chapter 15

The Hardest Hill

THE REMAINING HOURS OF THE LAST LEG of the voyage were spent in tranquility. I was commissioned to oversee the young Savannah Faith on her routine chores and duties. In a word, she taught me how *not* to keep a tidy ship and I taught her absolutely nothing at all. My time was spent with her just trying to keep up!

It was always a pleasure to be in the presence of such innocence and charm, "… a beacon in the darkness in the eyes of her pirate father," said he. I found it fascinating the way a beautiful mind works—she could be strolling in conversation about a lovely scarf her mother knitted for her then bluntly trail off to laugh about the night when her grumbling father tried to elude Shotglass Sam with a meal made of kelp. This happened apparently the night Sam had been caught drinking down the last of the captain's British ale. Savannah Faith once told me that the real treasures of life were ones of the heart, not discovered, dug for, or squandered. "You carry them with you always," she stated.

She spoke of the time when Sam was born, of how it makes her feel when her mother dotes over her while curling her hair. She even reminisced about a stampede of dolphins that were chasing the wind. As I listened intently to every word, I thanked the good Lord that there were people like her in this world.

Suddenly, a majestic blue whale barreled straight out of the water off the starboard rails. Fins up, it hung in mid air, timeless and stout before it playfully crashed down into the deep blue, smiling. The whole of it left me wide eyed and breathless. At that moment, I realized exactly what Savannah Faith had been talking about… and my heart soared.

With a strong wind at our back, it wasn't long before we saw land in the distance—the coastline of Jamaica and the shores of our salvation. We kept the ship at half canvas on the way into South Point with the hopes of an unannounced arrival as we hid in a shroud of evening fog. The closer we moved toward land, the more the island's beauty came into view. I saw lavish jungle lands that were rich with life and movement, painted seascape settings of amber and blue, cascading waterfalls in pools of emerald green that seemed to fall forever, and a row of gibbets hanging near the lighthouse at Mt. Airy, all of them swinging in time. Some were filled with dead pirates, some were not. Regardless, the message was a warning to all ruthless beggars and thieves that this land is governed.

The ship kept its course north, steady, as we still had to pass the seven mile stretch to get into Moonlight Bay. Our hopes were to find a seedy little hidey-hole in the wall called *Bowlegs Bight.*

Though another mythical landmark on the lips of pirates and sailors alike, Bowlegs Bight was rumored to be a place of enchantment by some, a place of mystery, grave, and voodoo by others. It was a fool's paradise—a land of superstition. Some say it was a place so righteous that it held the power to save a man's very soul or cast it aside into an eternity of time and punishment.

We drifted into Moonlight Bay like a band of gypsies, hungry and tired, searching for shelter. We were down but not beaten. We docked and calmly disembarked for the local village near Samsara to sniff around for clues that would help with our survival. No one paid us a nod as we strolled our parade down to the pier. That all changed the moment Barnacle Bill Bedlam emerged and made his descent—it was then that the coup began.

Suspicious eyes cut and fingers pointed while slurs and whispers gossiped around like a rum bottle passed from hand to hand. Apparently, Barnacle Bill's last visit on or near the island of Jamaica resulted in a hailstorm of gunfire, explosions and screams!

As curious eyes followed our captain, we moved as a horde knit tightly together, passing into the village always in search of the Spirit of the Sea. We thread our way through the townspeople to find *the one.*

"If you need answers to age old quests and queries, you must first find the eyes with the most wisdom," said Barnacle Bill Bedlam.

Our first stop was the stock for supplies. Yet, wherever we roamed, Bill Bedlam's reputation seemed to precede as the locals all looked at him as if he were a ghost. We made it about as far as the first doorstep when an elderly transient made the first offering. He was sitting idly by on the porch holding a pocket watch that he caressed in his hand, nervously rubbing the face of it with his thumb. An ex-military man-turned-vagabond was my guess by the looks of him. He appeared to be an old sailor that was out of money and out of luck. You could see the wear of hard, salty years in his eyes. His face was creased by time, every line told a story. Finally, after eyeing us for a time, the withered man spoke.

"It is V that you search for highwayman. Only she holds the power and the promise to stave a life of damnation… Barnacle Bill Bedlam!"

His mannerisms seemed odd as I watched the Barnacle give the stranger his best beguiling expression then with nothing more than a nod, he shied away and we moved on. We turned stones and shook branches along our path, but they all seemed to bear the same fruit and the name V rests on everyone's lips. Who is she? Will she really be an angel full of answers or will she be just another adversary sent by the Curse of Carbonados. We hung on every word from each wayward informant. Quite frankly, at that time, I didn't think I could weather another storm.

We moved up the Orange River towards the home of the one called V. I listened as echoes of strange calls from unknown birds filled the woods. This V wasn't too hard to find in actuality as fireflies lit a trail all the way to her door. The woman sat, waiting as if we had already arrived. She knew of our presence – she said she had seen us in the village. She claimed to have seen us as we awoke earlier in the morn!

Her name was Vyelula and we were instructed to pronounce each syllable separately as 'Vy-loo-la'. She had come to Negril by way of Baton Rouge onboard a merchant ship. She bled bayou in her blood—you could tell by her thick French accent. At her side was a large red bird—a Macaw she referred to only as Skully. I noticed the animal was handicapped, missing several toes from each foot. The bird struggled in its grasp so Vyelula would sit and feed him by hand a Cajun concoction of green apples and alligator pie.

She asked of Carbonados and the one called Malum with a voice thick with scorned, although a wisp of sarcasm penetrated her words. Meticulously, she studied the room—every wandering eye, every hand. She sat proudly and flashed a corrupt smile—a spider waiting for its fly. To say the least, the woman unnerved me—I couldn't figure her out.

When moonlight hit her eyes, she agreed to tell us everything—where to find Bowlegs Bight, who are the Circle of Souls, how to make contact with the very spirit of the Sea. Without taking a breath, she asked of compensation and the manner in which she would be paid.

"My essence comes at a price. Without me, you have nothing!"

The sea with all it's purity and grace protected her hidden trove of treasures, myths, and mysteries. She pointed a slender finger forward and added, "... from men just like you! These fares do not run gratis, the debt must be settled!"

On her word, Barnacle quickly became the center of attention by a clumsy fumble about in his pockets as if he were looking for something that was not there. V broke the awkwardness of the moment with the tone of voice.

"Put down your pence, Bill Bedlam. It carries no weight here. What I want from you is much more. Your amends with me must be squared by honor… your honor!" V stared right through Bedlam, an icy gaze that penetrated to his very core. "Would you spare a life for a friend?"

The Barnacle froze in step and looked at her. His chiseled eyes left no question that his undivided attention belonged to her. Shifting his temperament from a man who had just been seen humorously fumbling through his pockets, Barnacle Bill suddenly became more poised than ever as he graciously took a seat by Vyelula and smiled.

"I'm afraid I don't understand," said a puzzled Bill Bedlam.

Right then and there, the aura surrounding the woman melted. She became more somber and rested a hand on Barnacle Bill's sleeve.

"This world can be a very hollow place unless you have someone to fill it," Vyelula said and the words sounded like a prayer. "Truth be known I have not much time left in your world as I suffer a malignancy where there is no cure," she said and paused a moment. "I need a heart filled with good faith -- one of valor and virtue—someone to entrust my most cherished will."

The Barnacle raised a finger. "Are ya sure it's *me* you're looking for?"

His callas sense of humor knew no boundaries.

"I know who you are, Bill Bedlam," she

snapped. "When you were six years old, you found a small pouch of silver shillings left behind by some poor sod fresh off the town ferry. You kept not a piece of it for yourself. You spent every shilling on your mother, who had taken ill." She leaned back and eyed him before continuing. "At sixteen you saved your best friend from drowning... remember? He had been drinking and fell into the sea between the dock and the gangplank. His heavy clothing pulled him under in an instant. You snatched him from the water... and from death that night, didn't you?"

Captured by her stories, the room sat silent and still as she rambled on.

"In your thirty fifth year on this earth, you and your lovely bride Scarlett happened upon an infant, a newborn baby girl who had been abandoned by her mother. The child had health complications and was in need of attention. You sacrificed all that you had to get that bundle to the Royal Hospital in London. For days and nights on end, you stayed by her side. One of the hardest hills of your life came the day you left that hospital without her, was it not dear Captain?"

"That'll do!" growled the Barnacle with his eyes glazed in the candlelight. It seemed that he'd suddenly had his fill of reminiscing. "So what is this *cherished will* you speak of? And how may I help?" he said, attempting to change the subject.

"It's right in front of you," said V. "Right before your eyes, my one love, ma famille... Skully!"

The room was as still as a graveyard.

"You want me to keep the bird?" asked Barnacle.

I watched as a single tear trailed down her face as she spoke. "He's all I have in this world, all that I care for. I wish for you to take him as your own, give him love, let him know that his world is not a hollow place. Let him know that he's not alone." She turned away and whispered, "I will miss him dearly."

She knew she did not have long to live. It took every ounce of fight she had to keep the tears to herself—she was finally letting go. I watched as Vyelula faced *her* hardest hill.

The arrangement between the captain and V meant more to him than he dared to show, it was clear. Though the *cherished will* wasn't laced in silver, it held it's own beauty. The captain knew he could not mend her body but there was still a chance to heal her heart. Barnacle looked at her with just a smile and simply said, "Agreed."

Chapter 16

For Savior of Souls

WITH THE V'S WILL SATISFIED, WE MOVED on for the cure of Carbonados. She began to divulge with a short word of praise, "Pour sauveur des ames," which meant *"for savior of souls."* She was a woman of power, a mystic. She knew of the spell we were under but she could only offer words as guidance. She could go no further.

So we took her counsel and her parrot, and we were on our way. The last we heard as we parted ways was a gift that would one day prove useful. Vyelula confessed the bird was gifted with the power to heal in its touch. On its right hand—only one talon, "A hook." And that was all she said.

About two tics north of Moonlight Bay, about an hour at half sail, was where we would find Bowlegs Bight—concealed in the ruins of its fortress by the sea. A great and colorful wall of sea stone and larimar—the Caribbean waters' purest blue mineral—safeguards its mythical sanctuary from the world. It is also the burial site of its namesake, a pirate named Billy Bowlegs. As legend has it, Bowlegs was said to be the one man responsible for the demise of William Kidd. A rotten seed of a pirate, he hailed from the Dominican Republic and sailed on Kidd's last voyage to the Indian Ocean. He then sold Kidd out to Parliament upon their return. He too came to this hallowed place to see *MerAme* in hopes of saving his own soul... but he never made it past the wall.

We trudged around the grounds of the confines until we found a spot worthy to climb but Billy Bowlegs was not about to let us go so easily. The wall was weathered wet, covered in sea moss, and slicker than a whale's bottom. To climb it would not be an option offered to us.

We stumbled upon a bubbling mineral spring upwelling from the wall. Oddly enough, the flow defied the current. It's natural progression was not streaming away, the waters surge was instead swept back up under the wall as if it followed a stronger coarse. At closer look, traces of light sparkled in the pool from the other side. The Barnacle was convinced that he had found our passage, not over the grand wall... but under it!

I once read that 'crazy' was defined as odd, eccentric behavior, mentally deranged even. Bill Bedlam got more than his fair share as I saw the foolish glimmer in his eye—I knew the consequences were on the way.

He looked back at the Krewe with a smile, took

his hat in one hand, guns in the other, and in true swashbuckling style, jumped headfirst deep into the crystal blue spring. Within moments, Barnacle Bill disappeared under the wall.

The rest of us just stalled, staring at one another with a *who's stupid enough to jump next* look. Eventually we all followed suit, grabbed that last gasp, and dove into the deep blue unknown. Ours was a true case of 'monkey see monkey do'.

The very second I jumped into the water, I was sucked under quickly! The current was so strong that I didn't even have to swim. Like being shot from a drain pipe, the current gave us all a wild ride none of us would soon forget!

We emptied out of the channel, shaking like a pack of wet dogs—ragged and out of sorts, only to find Bill Bedlam laying on a beach, tanning himself in the sun. He looked peaceful with boots off, his hat a shield over his eyes. He lay there as if he'd been waiting for us far too long.

"Greetings Gents," he said. "You're looking rather flushed! I trust everything came out all right?"

I was certain I would find his banter a bit more amusing if it weren't for the fact that I had a mouth full of sand and sea salt. I wiped the salt water from my eyes and stared at him a moment. The scene was every sailor's dream: white sands, comfort, a tranquil blue balance of sea and sky over a secluded strand of beach. Rocks on both sides framed this stretch of unknown isle, making it nearly impossible to spot by anyone, even a passing ship. According to V, that was the location where we would find the Circle of Souls.

Sixty yards off shore was hallowed—where a timely gathering would regularly take place. We could walk out to it by sandbar since the water never got more than chest deep. That is, until we reached the reef, and then the bottom dropped out nearly five hundred feet straight down. That was where the Circle could be seen.

The Circle of Souls was made up of the spirits from the Haitian Tribe of the Holy that perished on the isle during the great hurricane of 1780. Every twelfth month, on the anniversary of the Tsunami, they would meet at the bottom of the sea in a courtyard of an isle that once was.

Call it what you like, be it prayer, ritual, or sacred remorse, they shed their fins for human form. The tribe would then come together in a circle and take each other by the hand, not to forget the calamity that had brought their world to an end, but to remember a good life that they had shared together. A tragedy claimed their very existence but it could not claim their human spirit… it lived on, even in the afterlife. Their sacred bond remained unbreakable. It is said that to experience the Circle, is truly heartening and holy—so much so that it attracts the daughter of Neptune herself, the Spirit of the Sea, MerAme.

So, we moved on to the sand bar out and went out where the water drew deeper around my waist. I began to think of how so few in life have ever really witnessed a treasure, the marvels of mother ocean… maybe even God himself. All of a sudden, I felt overcome, humbled, and almost spiritual. I didn't know how to act so I just kept walking on water.

Once out there, the reef's edge was beautifully marked by a floating bed of sea lilies. A playful pair of sea lions occupied the brush, playing a game of hide and seek. Affectionate and neighborly creatures, they took to flirting with the Krewe like old friends.

The Barnacle gently moved the lilies aside for a chance to better see down into the reef. Seconds later, the sea lions darted off in a hurry, like they were spooked. I feared that something bigger was coming.

In such an instance, nothing could prepare us for what came next. There were no wake up calls for miracles and *castles in the sky* that were once seen could not be forgotten. But beyond imagination and belief, if one would go a little bit further, he'd see exactly what my eyes saw that day.

The Holy Tribe had started to arrive.

The water there was pure aqua-marine, flawless and smooth. It magnified everything that laid in its garden like ants that are seen through a looking glass. We saw it all so clear.

From the shadows at the bottom of the reef, there was movement. Tall tails stirred in my peripheral vision and I knew I would need to be quick to catch a glimpse. I did see them though, as their souls rose from the coral. These creatures of the deep moved like the dolphin, agile and free to spiral in the shadows. Closer and closer they came.

It was amazing—the transformation was sharp. The moment their souls touched the sun they sprouted legs and walked into the sunlight as one enormous family—some young, some old. They were just as they had been in 1780. It all seemed so natural, watching them hug and kiss and smile with one another in remembrance, their bond had been unbroken. I, myself, could feel the warmth of their souls as they took each other by the hand. The whole of it left me smiling. One by one, they came together to form a circle and bow their heads in solemn prayer. The Circle of Souls was complete.

Never could any of us explain with any degree of accuracy or saneness the detail of what we saw in that moment... but there it was. Within the circle, a light shone from above—a bright, cylindrical beam that spotlighted the sacred garden on which they stood. Within that light, images flashed as others appeared. These were the images of their life from different periods of time—memories to tell the living of their people, a story to remind us of their legend. I watched the children play in a courtyard that appeared to be so real. I saw the fishermen skin the catch of the day to take home to feed their families. I saw their harmony... I saw their pain. The sublime light was so mesmerizing that it drew me in, as if I were actually present with them. I felt a commotion build. I felt the presence of their Savior coming... and maybe mine.

Their bodies began to cast an aura of green and blue. The colors spiraled above them, rising to the surface like a giant ring of sea-glass colored smoke, but it wasn't smoke at all… it was their souls… the Circle of Souls. The moment the ring of souls touched the water's edge, there came a blinding flash of light. Then suddenly, it was over. The light vanished and with it, the Holy Tribe. A last brief sighting flashed us as they disappeared from sight. Just like always, the ghosts would vanish, swimming deeper into the water before fading away.

Still half-dazed, I raise my eyes from the miracle just in time to feel my heart drop. We had been looking down for so long that we had no conscious idea that we had been found. She was already there… watching us watching them. I could not find breath in my body, I could not believe what I witnessed… it was a mermaid. As real as rain and just footsteps away from me, she sat atop her cornerstone, observing the outlanders within her secret garden by the sea.

Marble eyed and foolish I was. I embarrassed myself by dim-wittedly staring at her. Indeed, she embraced every ideology that the dreamer within me could conjure. A beautiful specimen of female… with a tail. Long flowing blonde hair and eyes of sapphire blue held me in her sight. So full of grace she was that I instantly wondered, *Could this be MerAme? Could this be the Spirit of the Sea?*

It seemed the moment of truth had arrived. The culmination and prospect of this cursed voyage, the fear, the anguish, the bad, the good – it had still foreseen hope to build promise upon this moment in time... in this place. To ask for a mercifully, granted wish from a celestial being such as she, the archangel of the sea... could it be possible?

With the decline of civilization and the hardships that reality can sometimes thrust upon humanity, it becomes very difficult to believe in anything anymore. Still, I believed and kept my dumbfounded gaze locked on the magnificent creature just the same.

She gracefully looked down at herself as she rested in the water, as if she were pondering a thought. Then with a swish of her tailfin, she wiped away her reflection and began to ponder about us.

"On what laurels brings you to this place? What faith do ye serve here, Sir?" She spoke and her voice was a song. It was clear, her only desire was to warrant our intentions as good. "... for reasons of my father's inquest," said she.

The Barnacle shot straight up and cringed as if a lightning bolt from Neptune's hand had already clutched him by the spine. Bill Bedlam found it a bit unnerving to know that Neptune, god of the sea world, god of earthquake and hurricane, counterpart of Poseidon, was aware of his intent. He and his curse, despair, and whereabouts lay exposed. It did not help that he still carried an ill temper!

Chapter 17

The Fire Devils

WITH THE WEIGHT OF THE WORLD UPON us, we had nowhere to run. We came for the Kuma-wani and prayed that MerAme would see fit to save our very souls. Suddenly, in my head, I heard the voice of Cygnus say, "Sin piedad. Sin piedad."

Life often had a peculiar way of showing it's worth, I never really knew what God had planned for me. Twenty years before the mast would be no matter, I wouldn't ever be ready for the final judgment. It paid to have a good captain, a man of good faith, and strong will. Mine was a captain who'd smile in the face of adversity, a captain who'd spit in the Devil's eye if need be.

Barnacle approached MerAme with respectful candor. "I come for my reckoning," he said. "I come to pay my dues! I know the fault of my wrongdoings. I've faced my crime! But I need the Kuma-wani to free my soul and the lives of my Krewe… the Skeleton Krewe." Then he bowed before her with honor to show his conviction.

I looked on in sheer disbelief, in awe as our

captain's honesty and somewhat tactless charm brought a smile to her lips. The next steps were indeed the longest. The wind had changed direction and the waves came at us without warning. It would appear that our divine intervention would have to wait a bit longer.

Rising from the deep blue depths, the scourge resurrected. From out of the water he came, standing atop the rippled waves of a reef five hundred feet deep. Lester was back for revenge—it would be the last stand.

He glided over water, toting his walking stick while smoking a fat cigar. With ease, he slithered his way closer to the rock where MerAme sat. Malum showed no mark, no esteem, no indifference to the Sea Spirit, the sacred waters on which he stood, or the powers that be. He had come for recompense and for no other reason. He was there to settle a score.

Lester called out across the still water. "I've come for the lambs… for souls to sacrifice. Our time of restitution is *now!*" His words growled deep enough to ripple the water. I felt my feet sink deeper into the sand bar that had become like quicksand. Something had its grasp on me… on all of us.

Within a light, my heart filled with promise. Nobleness, good grace, and prudence shone down upon us as the daughter of the god of all oceans, the spirit of this world's sea had taken a stand for my very life, and the lives of my captain and Krewe.

Her voice rang out sternly, proclaiming the law forthcoming and what would be.

"This insidious plague, any and all decree that empowers you, your warrant of contempt against Bill Bedlam and his Krewe is no more. It died with John Rackham," announced MerAme, "Your sovereignty and shame can no longer bind these men's souls for an eternity less served," she continued. "By Neptune's hand, these words shall be resolute!"

Her words did not sit well with the Medicine Man. I could see the backlash brew inside his pale lifeless eyes.

We'd reached a stand-off situation, an ill-fated status-quo. Never would I have thought that Wicked Lester's cunning would tempt him to be pitted against... a God. But what would I know? It seemed, the arrogance of evil had no bounds. The saying was true, "He who lives by the sword shall perish by it!"

In a rather haunting flash of déjà vu, the medicine man moved forward with his shiftless undertaking. He raised his hands in the air but spoke not a word, as my feet continued to sink deeper and deeper into the quicksand. With arms outstretched, he drew in the walking stick and lifted it to the sky, like a scepter, to draw power. The winds began to pick up and the waves crashed. Flames sparked from his cane in a flurry of lightning bolts while the squall around us intensified.

Suddenly, the dead rose.

Tommyknockers had returned and I witnessed the faceless disciples of Juan Carbonados. They moved ghoulishly, crawling like a crab up from the surf onto the sand. They crept closer as Malum's red fires lit up the sky. His war had been waged, a tempestuous battle of devilry and black magic appeared to have taken over. Strong southwesterly winds fanned the flames high into an inky sky above. *Convection spiral...* the 'Fire Devils' danced, just as the old timers had warned us. The firestorm encircled Barnacle Bill Bedlam, the Sea Spirit, and the rock upon which she sat, spitting out fire and debris in all directions.

By now MerAme's father was aware, this I

knew as I felt the ground I was stuck in begin to tremble and quake. On the horizon, a commanding display of power and force was witnessed by all as five vast water spouts approached us with blinding speed, side by side. Fueled by their master's rage and fury, a strength unstoppable, the wall of turbulent water would surely bury our souls and leave us washed away to lie dead in the sand. The end was near.

Out of the storm the voodoo man broke his silence as this whirling Fire Devil threatened MerAme, the Barnacle, and everyone else.

"La venganza es mia," he recited over and over. With every verse, his voice grew stronger. "*Vengeance is mine...* La venganza es mia."

There was one truth made known—vengeance would most surely arrive to deal a punch that no one would see coming.

The water spouts had almost reached us by then. The coast of Bowlegs Bight would never survive should the scourge reach its shores... and neither would we. I watched as doom and destruction fell around me. Yet amidst such horror, one thought filled on my mind with more choice words from my grandfather. They were both profound and obvious: *Never take the powers of this world for granted, appreciate the things you have and hold. Age is an illusion, eternity is a privilege that don't exist. Life's boundaries are fragile, fleeting. Live every moment vicariously 'cause the reality is... you're never gonna make it out alive!*

The last strike came. Wicked Lester cut his

eyes to the mermaid MerAme. He focused on pain. Drowning in a sea of malice and misplaced rage, his mind was bent on one thing—to satisfy the will of his Spanish tyrant father and the age old vendetta that haunted us.

Lester turned swiftly to advance his anger upon the Sea Spirit, but he didn't get far. In a fit of anger, he hastily charged right into the path of Captain Barnacle Bill and the thirty two inch, cold rolled steel saber that Bill had gripped tightly in his fist. The sinister smile emblazoned on his murderous face was quickly lost at the point of a sword. He had inadvertently stormed right into the blade, and as he did so, pierced the steel right through his abdomen.

The long awaited moment of vengeance had arrived.

For the first time, I saw something in Bill Bedlam I had never seen before. He stood there tall, statuesque, and frozen in his tracks. His body shook as he stood in place, It was an attack perhaps, not of fear but rather one of sweet retribution… of vengeance.

His next move was epic.

Lester slouched, wounded as he glanced down upon the sword that was stuck fast inside of him.

"Seize the moment," Barnacle said. In a glimpse of poetic justice the Barnacle leaned in closely to Lester's ear. With a low, raspy growl, Barnacle Bill Bedlam whispered, "Nos muestran sin piedad"—*we show no mercy*. Then, with years of torment behind his eyes, Barnacle drove that steel sword cleanly through his torso. I stood stunned and amazed, unable to move with my feet still stuck in the sand.

Wicked Lester pulled at the handle of his walking stick to expose a dagger hidden inside the cane. He bowed up with the intent to stab the Barnacle. Suddenly, his knees buckled under him as his body seized then turned rigid and still, like an old oak tree. Nothing moved, not even a finger.

Bold and brassy, the Sea Spirit dove at the medicine man to scratch his skin before crashing down under blue waters. From the legs up Lester's body begat to lose pigment. Gradually, his color changed to a sandy white—even his clothing lost its color. Marbled, his body glistened as it turned to sea salt. MerAme had cast her spell upon him, leaving him as a target for an even nastier fate. It was a strike of godlike measure.

The reef came alive. I could feel a presence moving in the deep dark waters below and I was scared to death! I couldn't see him but I knew he was there. God of thunder and lightning, god of wind and wave... Neptune would wait no more. He marked his path with fire and light that was brighter than a billion candles—a light as bright as heaven's gate, or so I assumed.

The discharge came with exactness and precision, instantly hitting it's quarry. His stone-salt body exploded on impact, blowing his brackish remains a hundred feet high. Grains of salt and ash swirled up to the heavens only to be engulfed by the oncoming band of water spouts. And he was gone.

As moments passed, the storm broke all around us then moved on, leaving no trace of its existence. I finally saw the sun again. MerAme returned to the sea with a splash, swimming straight to the same rock where Barnacle stood. With wonder, she looked him straight in the eye and placed her right hand over his heart.

"You saved my life, didn't you?" said the Sea Spirit.

For the first time, Barnacle Bill Bedlam had nothing to say. Instead, he just gave a worn out smile and held onto his pride. From the tattered pieces of netting that MerAme wore like scarves around her waist—the netting was adorned with small shells, trinkets, and curios that she had collected—she pulled a small doll-like figure. It looked like it had been hand carved from driftwood. It bared human resemblance but had shark-like features and a ragged feathered necklace that was tied around it's neck.

It was the Kuma-wani, right there in her hand.

I'd been waiting the entire dark voyage to see it… to see if it was real, to see if this whole damn trip was real. The men had been waiting longer. It is said that when man finally meets the Divine, God's image is so great—much too intense for the human mind to behold—so the experience is perceived as something from memory, something familiar—a trick to help mortal minds better comprehend. In my case, the Spirit did not use imagery—instead she used her word. It was praise that we all knew too well.

The Spirit of the Sea placed her right hand over Bill Bedlam's heart and with a genuine smile, she passed the Kuma-wani on to our captain. As she gently folded his hand around the talisman, she spoke words that would save our lives.

"Pour sauveur des ames, Pour sauveur des ames," she said with her hands clasped tightly around the amulet. *For savior of souls,* she'd said and I saw the ocean's daughter smile back at me.

As suddenly as we had found her, she took to the waters and was out of sight. It was then that I had realized... we were free. Our curse had been lifted, the nightmares of Carbonados were over.

Chapter 18

Words like Whiskey

WE RETURNED TO THE SHIP WITH OUR souls intact and a desire to leave the shores of Jamaica behind. Throughout all the adventures and for as long as I have known Bill Bedlam, I still find it heartening to see him reunite with his wife and child. The life of a pirate is dangerous and daring – one never really know what lies beyond the horizon. Every sunset must be savored.

Like any good father, Barnacle returns with a gift in hand. Barnacle treasures his daughters surprised reaction to Skully, the bird he had cleverly tucked behind him.

I don't know why, but I took notice of a mark on the outside of Boo's wrist. At first, it looked like a cat scratch, nothing much, a typical malady for any kid. The Barnacle put Skully down on deck as Boo tapped on the wood planks for his attention. The bird called out "C'mere!" and I watched as the big red parrot waddled his way straight for her. He crawled onto her hand, bobbing his head for affection as she began to dote on him. You could almost see a bond of trust form between them. I smiled as I watched them. Then suddenly, I got spooked by a feeling—it was as if I'd been hit in the face with words. *The power to heal in his touch,* rang the voice of Vyelula in my head. I watched as Savannah handed the beautiful bird over to her mother Scarlett. The moment the bird left her hand the mark had vanished, the scar was gone. No one else caught it... but I did.

With a clear conscience and the Kuma-wani in our possession, we turned our sails for home. The long road was traveled and it's purpose had been amended. Days go by with nothing but calm waters, blue skies, and bliss as we sailed away for the safe harbors of homeland. Though our purses were empty and did not jingle with coin, our profit was much greater—we got our lives back.

As we drew nearer to port, I could clearly see the lights of Sadie's Ol' Mill Tavern glow in the distance, guiding us in like the old sailor's tall tales—ghost stories told by those who boast and brag. It gave me a chill.

As we drifted closer, I saw Sadie herself stand at the waterfront, looking as if she knew we were set to arrive. She wasn't alone. There was a lady at her side who looked familiar. Georgia—the lady whom I had helped with her baggage so long ago. She seemed distraught, almost hysterical, weeping and waving her hands in the air as if she had seen a ghost. Perhaps... she had. She never took her eyes off the ship. She studied it's coarse all the way into the slip, following along as she made her way down the boardwalk, as best as her legs could keep up.

In the long wait I considered what a treat it would be to beat my feet in the green grass of home with the feeling that I cheated death once more, dodged another bullet, lived to see the day… I survived. I couldn't help but question, *was it all meant as the sign of a good pirate or just dumb luck that saved my skin? I guess we'll never know.*

I could almost hear Georgia's voice cry out from the wharf. I followed the sound through a cluster of blank faces, anxious to see what was troubling her. When I finally found her in my view, within earshot, the wind carried her words and stung at my memory, a tug at my heartstrings for hope. She looked past me, the tears flowing down her face, and said, "My Son… That's My Son!"

She pushed her way through the folk until she got her hands on the one person she sought out. I stood there rattled and confused, but I never took my eyes off the sweet ol' gal. I watched as her world came full circle. The years of prayer, kindred hope, and strong belief wasn't for naught. The only thing she had ever had in this world had come back home.

She wrapped her arms around her only child—Morgan the Hook. Abruptly she pulled the hat from his head and started to caress his face with her hands, like a sculptor forging in clay. But we all know why she had to touch him so—to see if he was real or if he was just the miscue of an aging mind and a broken heart that played tricks on her. She kept calling him Eddie. "My little Eddie," she said as she held onto him with all her might.

As I stood there, scratching my head, trying to picture Morgan the Hook as her British Admiral son, the answer I sought came from somewhere over my left shoulder. "Edward Creekmore," the voice said. "Admiral Edward Creekmore of her Majesty's Royal Navy... formerly." I turned to find Barnacle Bill Bedlam staring at me, offering the explanation. "After a hero's service, Morgan found that a life governed wasn't a life at all so he took a course for freedom, for piracy," said the Barnacle. "Sadie told me of Georgia. For many moons I've known the truth. For many moons I've tried to get him to come here. But for fear of reason and the hangman's noose, we had no choice but to stay away, you see." He paused a moment and gazed off toward the sea then continued softly, "I never told you... I never told anyone really!" confessed the good captain. "Everyone of us in life must follow his heart on whatever course it might lead him. It's destiny, a calling." He looked sternly at me. "By design, you have the power to forge a legacy, to prove your very existence in this world. It's not about success or failure, whether you win or lose, it's about the journey and life's lessons offered along the way. Be it blessing or burden, life is what you make it, every living soul has a cross to bear."

The credo spoken by Captain Bill Bedlam was humbling and right on the mark. I realized that truth, as I caught myself staring at a tear-filled overwrought Georgia, rediscovering a son she had thought she had lost so many years ago.

In life, many fall self-involved, blinded by shiny things, decadence, and money. People lose sight of life's true worth, those things that lay closest to the heart. As I came of age, those colors became more clear and I started to see God's world in a different light.

With my mind a bit clouded in musings, I noticed Barnacle Bill favoring one side—his shirt tail was tattered and stained in blood. I could tell he was in pain from the shark bite he had suffered.

Impishly I teased, "Did that hammerhead get the best of you?" I said it jokingly, trying to make light of the situation. Suddenly, his face dropped and he paused in silence, like the cat had got his tongue. I saw Miss Scarlett stand there, hiding her school girl smile, grinning but politely trying not to show it only to arouse my suspicions all the more. I was doing my best to man up and not hark back into being… me, blinding him with my juvenile nonsense and demand.

The beautiful Scarlett leaned over the Barnacle's right shoulder, nudging at her pirate husband to whisper him on. He kept to himself in silence. Finally, to break the ice, Boo sharply broke from her mother's hip and smacked the Barnacle on the bum, right on the side where his wound lay, lighting him up with pain. He gave out a hair-curling scream that ended in two words, "GATOR TRAP!" Now, the captain's eccentric conduct had always kept me off balance, and this was no exception. It would seem that I'd been sorely misled. His painful admittance came with a fuss.

"The Shark never bit me son," he said with a sigh. "It brushed my tailcoat, gave me a wink of the eye, and off it went! Truth be known, on board the ship is a twelve year old bottle of Shepherds Rum, underhandedly hidden by one Morgan the Hook. When the ship started to capsize during the storm, I felt a bit whipped and I figured it as good a time as any to have a hearty strong snifter. Sometimes you must stoke the fire to keep the kettle brewin', savvy? So I made my way for the Shepherds, thinking Morgan was none the wiser. Come to find out, he had his sweet spot rigged with a gator trap or *kitty chasers* as we used to call them! The moment the ship went down I was washed off my feet and fell backwards onto the bottle and trap. The bottle broke, the trap jaws triggered and snapped shut on my backside, locking on to my bum like a rabid dog… or gator." We both began to chuckle as his confessions continued. "I broke my sword off trying to pry it loose," laughed Barnacle Bill. It was a nice moment we both shared, smiling.

I looked out over the faces of those that survived. Who has seen what I've seen? Bloody Bob and his men, scarred but strong. I saw Hawkeye and Turtle Brit, cracking into the last bottle of sacrificial wine. Morgan and his mother had moved on. Miss Scarlett and Boo seemed to have faded from sight. The Krewe had dispersed for the Ol' Mill Tavern and the cool drinks that awaited them there. Just two of us were left, standing together as he began to share his final sermon.

"Nothing in life is as it appears to be, Mr. Bones… nothing. And first impressions are fallbacks of the foolish. We live in one realm, one big game of chance, I hope you play your hand well!" The Barnacle's words soaked in like whiskey, skillfully aged and with all good intention, though it still burns going down.

"The world has its fill of uncertainties," said

he. "Don't let a noose of darkness and negativity hang you! Paint your life full of color and you'll sail through it smiling, or as my dear Scarlett loves to say, 'Learn to dance in the rain.' You'll find the life you seek, you'll find peace for a restless soul, if you follow the call of your heart... the heart of a pirate. It'll cure what ails ya!" he said, smiling. "Like I said, *"words like Whiskey."* He grinned and continued, "Belay common sense, truth be known, in my case anyway... it really ain't that common. Most of all, live your life without regret, young man. Remember there's no such thing as second chance. Be of good heart and be brave, the life of the foolhardy is lonesome... but free."

I reeled in the guidance, yet hung onto every word. I had no reason for doubt—his influence had kept me alive, and that's no lie! As I listened to his words, my mind drifted into a surreal state. A rush of memories had returned to join me and I couldn't seem to shake them. Distracted, I found my eyes grounded by one place, one spot of land, I could see it clearly—the rickety old fence post where it all had begun. It was the one I had straddled in waiting when my life changed direction. I knew it well!

Suddenly I was jarred from my jaded imagination. I could hear the sound of the mystic foghorn whistle blow, signifying the end of the day and I lost my place. I turned to find Barnacle Bill Bedlam had gone. He'd vanished in a glance, like in my memory, leaving nothing but a glimmer—the trademark of a good pirate.

It wasn't until moments later that I realized just what he was talking about. What could be construed as menial task and direction to me was invaluable. No preachment, chalk talk, or aimless ramblings. This was my life, my prospect, my fortune. It was meant to be a lantern to light my path, a helping hand for when I fall. No longer a sinner in a sin, I had a friendly reminder that I was free. It was plain to see… the treasure was mine.

Although it didn't rattle and glisten like a plate covered in gold doubloons, its shine was brighter than any fist of gold. I had my life back, my soul, my future.

As I stared off at my beautiful harbor, a light summer rain started to fall over me, cleansing my soul.

I smiled as I looked out over the water. I could finally see the rainbow through the rain… and I thought of my pirate friends.

Then, I started to dance.

The End

About the Author

THEY SAY HISTORY IS WRITTEN BY THOSE who make the wake!

The mystery or saga behind the man named Barnacle is perplexing. His pirate blood runs thick as does his thirst for adventure.

Rumors of his upbringing span from the sands of the Gulf of Mexico to the backwoods of Virginia… and everywhere in between.

He tells that he's wrestled alligators and even slept in the same bed with a fourteen foot Burmese python named Gwendolyn.

He has walked with stars on western shores and shared the limelight for many years with his song.

It was in a Tavern on the North side of Babylon where he met his soul mate.

With golden hair and eyes of crystal blue waters, she has a smile as warm as a Florida sunset. He knew the moment he laid eyes on her that his world was complete, and so they sailed away.

Charting a course eastward in search of a home, settling down, they dropped anchor in a small province off the coast of Carolina… and then came Boo—another pirate in the fold. The Barnacle is a proud papa of his brown eyed girl. She's the captain's confidant, powder monkey, master trainer of the Barnacle's parrots and one heck of a dancer.

With the wind in their hair, the family took stride, carving their mark on new frontiers. From the badlands to the coastal waters, the Barnacle still roams free—his whereabouts unknown.

Through all the years and miles, the tears and smiles.

One love, one life… Pirate.

Famous Last Words from the Barnacle

I climb aboard my soapbox one last time for the good…

Don't wait for second chance, it may never come. Live for the dream, live your life to the fullest… you only have the one.

There is more to this world than the drudgery of daily grind. You must find it, seek it out, whatever the whim that fulfills you and keeps your heart young.

You and only you possess the power to make your world a better place, it's true beauty cannot be seen by living in a box.

Take pride in all the madness of a creative mind and try to keep your heart free as a child, feet never touching the ground.

Remember a tide of prosperous dreams, one little wave could last forever.

And always… leave room for wonder. It's true! The power of imagination fuels the human spirit in us all… without it we would be lost.

Good Fortunes

I would like to thank everyone who played their part in bringing my dreams to reality.

I would like to thank the BOC.

To Kim Ellis, aka *Kaliope Kim.*

The pirate consultant and my saving grace – the only rogue who could make heads or tails of such a fine mess of ramblings!

You were one of my first pirates and one of my last. I shall always remember… friends 'til the end!

To Joe, *Morgan the Hook*

You have always been my friend of fortune, this story is yours. I'll salute you always as Pirate Lord of the Brethren of Caroline and I'll be your friend through storms or sunshine 'til we reach our destiny.

To Arthur Whittam, aka *Cascabel*

Thank you my friend for letting me share your likeness and your spirit for the character Cygnus. You truly do show wisdom in your eyes (or maybe it's because I'm looking at you through the glass bottom of my tankard… again!) You're the pirate's pirate, you carry my respect wherever you go.

To the Mermaid, *Sati DeMayhem*

You couldn't be more perfect for the daughter of Neptune. You have the spirit of the sea in your eyes, the powers to captivate… I sincerely thank you.

To the talented photographers Mike McSunas at Legendary Photography USA

"You Da Man"… you got my Clint Eastwood shot and to JS (you still know who you are).

To my Family

You are my sun and my moon, my star to steer by. You hold my heart in your hands.

Faith

"Now and then we had a hope that if we lived and were good, God would permit us to be Pirates."

~ Mark Twain

The Tales

of

BARNACLE BILL

Continues to sail on...

keep your eye on the horizon!

CPSIA information can be obtained
at www.ICGtesting.com
Printed in the USA
FSOW03n1358180816
23945FS